C.S. Boag is a former journalist who has also grown potatoes, driven taxis and bulldozers and worked in a hamburger bar. He has travelled many times throughout Australia and to France, speaking enough French not to die there. He was a Sydney City Councillor for six years and holds degrees from NSW and Sydney universities as well as postgraduate qualifications from Macquarie. Besides publishing short stories he has also worked as a columnist for *Woman's Day* and the *Bulletin*. He won the Walter Stone Memorial Prize for Literature in 1986. C.S. Boag lives on a small 'green' holding near Bathurst, NSW, with his wife, Judith. He has five children.

www.csboag.com

By the same author

The Case of The Hood With No Hands

C.S. Boag

MISTER RAINBOW

in the Case of the

DEATH OF A LADIES' MAN

XOUM PUBLISHING

Sydney

First published by Xoum in 2013

Xoum Publishing
PO Box Q324, QVB Post Office,
NSW 1230, Australia
www.xoum.com.au

ISBN 978-1-922057-53-2 (digital)
ISBN 978-1-922057-54-9 (print)

Cataloguing-in-publication data is available from the
National Library of Australia

Word count 50,200

For Sophie, Gemma, Max, Zola, Escher,
Matilda, Wolfe and Carter

*If you don't mind your own business in this world, some
joker's going to come along and mind it for you.*

Chapter 1
STIFF LUCK

It's the winter of our discontent. There's no ice on the streets of Sydney town but there's plenty in the veins of the hitmen. And I reckon there's ice of a different kind in the track-riddled arteries of the junkie sidling past the fresh-minted corpse in the gutter.

The corpse is neatly parked, all lined up with the kerb nice and tight. It's a well-constructed cadaver, the sort you'd enter in a Mr Corpse competition, if they ever had such a thing, and it was yours to enter. The thing is, this particular corpse doesn't possess a head. Feet, legs, torso, arms, hands, neck – but no head.

An hour or so earlier, while I was busy bailing out my boat, the *Wooden No*, a dame called Annabel Franklin phoned on one of my dead-men's mobiles. She was worried for the safety of her lover because a person or persons unknown were out to kill him. Annabel saved my life when my nemesis Pandora tried to fold me on the cusp of the caper I filed away in the locker labelled 'SUN' – that's Solved Until Further Notice – aka The Case of The Hood with No Hands. Accordingly, I owed her one, so I quit bailing, climbed down into the scow and rowed myself across the wine-dark sea. I then bussed my way into Megalopolis and hoofed it to the pointy end of town . . .

But I'm too late – somebody's *lifetime* too late – and the remains of Annabel's lover are enjoying the siesta that never ends in a gutter in a side street in that salubrious part of Sydney town known as Kings Cross.

I squat and make the first of my observations: the body is togged-out nice and neat in jeans and T-shirt, albeit lightly blood-spattered.

I calculate the armament employed to be in the elephant-safari category – with the accent on *gory* – small enough for a well-built joker to tote under a three-quarter coat, but big enough to blow a pachyderm's brains out. It was sufficient to knock off this joker's skull, anyway.

Position of assassin: Directly to the fore of the victim.

Angle of fire: More or less head-on.

Distance of muzzle from phyzog: Somewhere around zero-range, or point-blank in the old money.

Executive summary: Someone didn't like him.

So what's new? To have known this joker was not to like him. Thomas L. Tycho was everybody's enemy, a trickster who played one trick too many on one too many people, a dirty dealer who dealt one dirty deal too far, a wide boy wide enough to keep himself alive until the moment he made the mistake of wide boys the world over – not getting a whole lot narrower when the gun went off.

How do I know all this? I'm not a detective for nothing, unless you're talking about what they pay me.

I shoot a Captain Cook along the boulevard and note three more items of interest.

One: It's a fine day.

Two: It's Kings Cross, so punters are passing by on the other side of the street in order to maximise their chances of enjoying said fine day.

And three: Both sides of the boulevard possess blank walls – one of them newly decorated with blood – thereby providing no convenient viewing platform for the delectation of witnesses to a murder.

I ascertain all this before the cops rock up, with just enough time left over to catch up on a little light reading, kindly provided by the corpse in question. The words are in a ring-a-rosy conformation around the headless honcho's neck – right below where the fuse box neatly carved off his entablature – the sort of tattoo someone might wear in place of an inscription on a T-shirt, just to let you know what kind of guy he is, all the while relieving himself of the time-wasting business of small talk.

That's how I know the body belongs to Thomas L. Tycho. I can't see all of the tattoo – Tommy's lying on his back and the punchline's busy talking to the tar macadam – but I know from memory how it goes, and how it goes is as follows:

Populus vult decipi – ut falleret . . .

No trouble with the translation, thanks to my Aunt Rube. She taught me Latin, along with how to shoot a gun, how to move, how to withstand pain, plus a whole lot of other critical points about the private detecting business.

The people wish to be deceived – so deceive them.

I straighten just as the police sirens wind up the decibels, while the pedestrians churn by on the other side of the street like they think they can escape Destiny – all they got to do is look the other way.

'It says –' comes a female voice from behind me.

I turn around, fast. Annabel, the dame who just phoned, has appeared out of nowhere wearing an expression of pure horror on her dial-up and a frock that's hiding about as much as a wet bikini at Bondi Beach.

'I know what it says,' I say. 'What I want to know is why he put it there.'

Annabel looks incredulous. 'Oh, that's easy. Tommy always liked to make out he was smarter than everybody else. He –'

But if there's any more to an answer that's making as much sense as a law and order editorial in *The Daily Terrorgraph*, I'll have to put it on hold. The rozzers are hurtling around the corner of William and Hackberry, Glocks in their fists, justice in their eyes; the pockets of their blue serge playsuits bulging with unused ammunition.

'We need to find the emergency exit,' I say.

'But what about –?'

'Look, your Tommy might not be going anywhere but that don't mean we have to go there with him. Like the man in the poem says – we got to keep our heads while all about are losing theirs.'

There are three ways of dealing with situations like this: come out with your hands up and buy yourself a one-way ticket to the goosepot; take your chances and go down in a fusillade of arrows; or join the pedestrians.

I choose number three: life. I grab Annabel's hand – which is still rough with the scars from where she crushed out the Edison the night she saved me from certain death in the speakeasy – tip my fedora to the corpse, then dart into the foot traffic heading towards the Coca-Koala sign at the Top-of-the-Cross, all the while pretending to engage in meaningful dialogue.

'I'm Smith, by the way.'

Cop cars nail the street fore and aft and enough persons in uniform emerge to start another war in Afghanistan.

She looks at me in surprise. 'Smith? Well, shouldn't we stay and help the police?'

'Lady, if we hang around any longer, we'll shoot straight to the top of these doozies' target list. Besides, there's no need for an ID when the corpse already carries a toe tag, even if it *is* situated at the wrong end of its anatomy. Wearing a necktie like the one he's got, your boyfriend doesn't need collaring. Some deaths go straight to the Unknown Victims department, but this one's what you might call a no-brainer.'

Chapter 2
BECAUSE OF THE STAIRS

The hand in mine goes tense – past and present tense, but a little shaky on the future. I figure I better elaborate. 'Look, *no-brainer*'s just an expression, okay? It doesn't mean – given Tommy's current condition – that I'm making him the butt of a bad gag. So let's just look straight ahead and keep walking.'

Annabel does like she's told, and I do what's necessary to keep her mind off an horrific situation. I ask her why she phoned me.

'Because Tommy said they were out to get him. It was the last thing he told me before leaving the club this morning. I knew something bad was going to happen and I also remembered the card you gave me so that's why I called you. Tommy must have gone away and come back again because it' – she shudders – 'it happened just half an hour later.'

'Did he say who?'

'Who what?'

'Who was out to get him.'

She shakes her head. 'No, he just said *they*. There were so many people who, you know, *hated* Tommy. It was all building up to a Ganymede.'

'You mean Runnymede.'

Annabel shrugs. 'Whatever. Anyway, the killer could have been anyone.'

Out of the corner of my gizmo I notice a cop taking a step in our direction. 'Hey, youse!'

I slow the pace. Do more than stroll and the rozzer will laser us. He might also beat us to death and tell the Police Integrity Commission we were running from the scene of a decapitation and he was therefore duty bound.

'Where do you lay your head?' I ask Annabel.

'What do you mean?'

'Hang out, reside, dwell, lodge, doss down, domicile.'

She tells me an address in Macleay Street.

'Okay, Anagram, you take the high road and I'll take the low, and I'll see you at your place in five.'

That's when we part company. That's also when the rozzer discovers that the plural form of the second-person pronoun isn't working for him any more, because me and Annabel have split into two singulars, so he shelves his Glock and goes back to doing what he's paid to.

The high road takes Annabel up to fairyland while the low road takes me into that part of the world known as Woolloomooloo (which could be a public convenience for livestock but instead is an expensive piece of Sydney real estate). The 'Loo lies beneath the shadow of a cliff that's darkened by the deeper shadow of too many unanswered questions. For example: How come the killer blew off Tommy's head so neat it was like a dotted line joined it to the rest of the body? And: How come the death occurred *after* I received notification, and not before, in the manner of most heinous crimes?

I chuck a shooftee around me as I turn up the McElhone Stairs. No one's following, if you don't factor in my imagination. The McElhone Stairs – a hundred or so rough-hewn slices of Sydney mother rock worn lower than a Sister of Mercy's hemline – take you from the 'Loo up to Potts Point. I'm a long time reaching the top. And even longer by the time I'm hoofing it across Victoria Street and along the nefarious back alleyways. Eventually I reach a brown-brick hostelry with a dinky little alcove nursing a dozen or so green security buttons. I enter via the grille door, and ring Annabel's ding-a-ling – in the only way I'm ever likely to.

But there's no answer.

Thanks to the McElhone Stairs, some *fifteen* minutes have elapsed, instead of the agreed-upon five, giving Annabel time to prepare herself for my arrival. So why isn't there some kind of response?

The hostelry is pre-war but it's had a facelift that includes a new blanket of paint, a wheelchair ramp, and a sign that says 'Hawkers Can Go To Buggery'. After I've considered all of the above, I thump the button with 303 next to it again, before trying 403 instead. That would be the apartment directly above 303.

'Yes?'

It's a dame, only it's not my dame.

I say I'm the postman, with a special delivery.

'Stick it in the letterbox.'

'Too big for the letterbox.'

'Dump it on the floor.'

'Not safe on the floor.'

There's an audible sigh. 'All right, I suppose you'd better come up.'

The lock on the security door clicks me in. The elevator is an old Otis, and its mirrored cabin walls tell me I'm much the same as when I last looked – a broad-shouldered, hammer-fisted joker something over the six-foot mark in the old money, clad in green-striped daks, a red-houndstooth jacket, and the sort of footwear they used to call 'correspondent's shoes', but which I call whitesides. My peepers are set in a phyzog that looks like it's gone more than a couple of rounds with a cage full of gorillas, and they're staring hard-eyed out at a bleak world from under a yellow chequerboard fedora.

But it's not me I'm interested in, it's Annabel Franklin, and the instant the Otis disgorges me I scoot along a short hallway decorated with a mangy carpet towards a door that's book-ended with a garbage chute and an escape hatch. The number beside the doorknob reads pretty much what I expected it to read: 303.

The hatchway's shut, so I give it a Mike Hammer.

The answer's a great deal of silence.

Chapter 3
ROOM 303

I'm all for the quiet life. That's why I've got no means of identification – no private inquiry licence, no driver's papers, no usurer's card, no phone except for the twenty or so dead-men's mobiles Rory palmed me, no email addresses apart from the ones I borrow from the unwary, no tax file number, and no real estate. At least that anyone knows about.

My address might be fixed, but it's fixed only by a frayed, one-inch hempen hawser knotted to an anchor buried in the sands of an out-of-the-way hidey-hole in Sydney Harbour. The other end of the rope's attached to a tub that only just avoids joining the anchor because of a semi-reliable bilge pump, and a lot of bailing. My boat's an old clinker-built ferry called the *Wooden No* – at least that's what I tell jokers that want to know more about my domestic arrangements than can be good for anyone, most of all me.

'What's the name of your boat?' they ask.

I just say *Wooden No.*

Why do I need to stay under the radar? Because people are after me – crims; cops; an ex-wife; the tax man; jokers that for one reason or another either hate me or want money I haven't got; the odd identity thief; and Pandora.

Who's Pandora? Tell me the answer to that and we'll both know. All I can say is she's a killer with just one thought in the brainpan behind that horribly scarred face of hers, and that's to kill me. Pandora's the main reason I choose to go through life incognito. She's also the main reason I nearly found myself dead after getting to the bottom of the Handless Hood caper. But that's another story.

In this story I'm standing outside Annabel Franklin's apartment door just like I was told to do when I hear something.

And it's only after I've been listening too long that I realise what that something is.

It's nothing.

When a dame in distress is waiting, you expect to hear *some* sort of noise, even if it's only a coffee machine gurgling in the scullery, the flush of a water closet, or the barely-discernible purr dames make when they're applying their make-up. But right now the dust mites under my whitesides are making more noise than Annabel, and her silence can only mean one of two things – she's either not home, or she's dead.

The apartment door gives at the first nudge of the shoulder protector. It's a watermelon of a thing made of pastry flakes and bum fluff, with a lock that might have been snipped off the innocent head of a premature neonate with sugar scissors. My hard-heft roll takes me along a hallway into a drawing room that's long since ceased to be used for drawing in and instead is your usual shrine to the computer age. I clock a table propping up an AWA television, a TEAC hi-fi, a Compaq laptop saying it's got Windows 7, and the sort of printer you get for next to nothing from your local post office.

Television: Off and cold.

Hi-fi: Ditto.

Printer: Ready and waiting.

The laptop's got a dinky little sign on it saying words to the effect of: WHATEVER WAS ON THIS SCREEN IS CURRENTLY OFF IN LA-LA LAND, PRESS ANY KEY TO CONTINUE.

I do like it says but I don't hang around for the results. Instead, I haul out the Smith & Wesson Compact and scope the rest of the joint, in order to check up on the silence.

The kitchen's one of those alcoves that even the most self-deluded of real-estate mohickeys would sticky-tape an *-ette* on the end of. It features a cupboard that'd explode if you tried to cram anything bigger than a tea cup in it; a dinky single-plate floater-stove; a fridge that would require a cyclist's dose of hormones to qualify as anything more than an ice bucket; and a sink on which someone has left a knife.

The brass plaque on the half-open door next to the kitchen features a lady's leg and the words *Salle de Bain*. Behind the door is the kind of scent Cleopatra might have worn to hang onto Egypt, a mix of Nile delta and rainforest with intimations of halcyon mist and desert mirages – but none of the odours you might describe as bodily.

Lime-green bathtub: Empty.

Lime-green hand basin: Wiped clean of all evidence of human occupancy.

Lavabo: Seat down and shining, a roll of lavatory wipes neatly hidden in the long blue skirts of a ballet dancer perched atop the cistern.

I hear a sound like a door opening and go into a crouch followed by a half-spin, gat at the more-than-ready. But it's only the laptop, its little bell advising it's finally come out of sleepy time and all I need to do is press any key to continue. But there's one more room to check before I do that. In my experience, if you leave one more room to check, it's more than likely to jump out when you least expect it, and check you.

The sign on the door says *Couchez.*

I take it as an invitation, bang open the door and enter.

Pink carpet.

Padded pink chair with purple flowers on it.

Pink dressing table, complete with powder-pink brush-and-comb set.

Pink built-in and pink curtains opening onto a day that's far too lovely for anyone to die in.

But tell that to the Fates, because the Fates are telling me – via the cerise-framed mirror in the built-in – that on the pink-quilted bed sprawls the body of a beautiful dame who has died on this most beautiful of days. And I know for a fact when she died, because I was in her company no more than twenty minutes prior.

It wasn't a natural death. I can tell that by the look on Annabel's face, the fact that the clothes that hid nothing before are hiding even less now, and because the hole in the region of the heart isn't standard-issue, and could only have been made by the knife that the murderer left on the sink in the kitchenette.

Annabel saved my life but I've let someone take hers. I gave her one of my dead-men's phone numbers but it was either not enough or too much to stop someone killing her.

I lift the pink-quilted dressing gown from the foot of the bed and pull it gently up, being extra careful with the scars on the hands she got when she saved my life.

Suddenly I can't see too good and the Scene-of-Crime boys can read the subsequent cover-up any way they want to.

I get the hell out of the pink room.

Chapter 4
THE DAME PACKS A GAT

The Compaq's waiting so I do like it says and smack the tab marked ENTER and the screen coughs up . . . a list of names – no capitals and no punctuation, just a list of names and most of them badly spelt – like they were written by someone with only a couple of minutes to write them in.

While I'm waiting for the printout I run through the sequence of events that ended in Annabel's demise, like they do on one of those old James Cagney movies Aunt Rube used to screen on the dining-room wall of my childhood, with Rube telling me: *Watch this and now this – all right, now tell me what might have happened after he died.*

I see Annabel hurrying away to her destination with death, taking the high road just like I told her to, the one that passes all the strip joints and the places selling genuine Australian mementos manufactured in The People's Refulgence of China, the road that was supposed to not have any shadows in it but does – just the one. And that one shadow follows Annabel from the scene of the crime with its hood up only a few paces behind her – because that's what shadows do. It bypasses the prostitutes with the too-short skirts and the cold sores, and the touts and the beggars and the druggies. It then works its way along the mean streets still following the dame with the ruby-red lips – because that's also what shadows do, particularly ones intent on killing people.

Annabel gets herself in through the grille door – fumbling for her key to the security hatch – clicks open the lock and hurries inside, slamming the door fast because she senses the Fates are fast closing in on her. She presses the button in the Otis that will convey her to the third floor, alone in the lift except for her fears, and the multiple images of the ashen-faced woman in the skimpy attire reflected back by all the mirrors around her.

The printer's making a noise like it's being strangled so I whack a few buttons and it finally starts to produce the goods. At the same time the intercom crackles into life, followed by someone saying *Police here!* in the sort of voice that suggests it's not going to be there much longer.

I get myself fast into the kitchenette, lean down and smell the knife handle. All it tells me is the hand that wielded the weapon that killed Annabel Franklin was wearing a Mediflex surgical glove. Back in the lounge room, I grab the printout, rip out the electric Fords and head for the hatchway, shoving the papyrus into a skyrocket, tucking the laptop under my armpit as I go. I'm too late to make good my escape in the traditional manner, because as I get to the landing the lift-gates are already whanging shut like the steel-barred doors of a maximum-security prison and the grinding of the elevator gears are the machinations of the law.

I hear shouts and the thump of police-issue boots.

The shooftee I chuck around the corridor reveals a little glass eye staring at me from the apartment at the other end, an arrow telling me the Otis is heading my way, a door with a green man on it indicating the exit, and the garbage chute. I chuck the glorified typewriter down the slippery slide, settle the fedora, and as the elevator shudders to a stop, step into the fire escape.

Now, there are two types of fire escape – ones that are there for escaping fires by and ones that are there to die in. This one's the second type, with pot plants against the cracked-concrete walls, black bags of rubbish on the horizontals and mouldy food busy feeding an army of cockroaches. You'd be better off taking your chances with the fire.

A wardrobe blocks the downward passageway, but that's not the one I'm taking as I hurdle a pile of garbage bins, my whitesides clickety-clacking on the steps as I hear the lift door opening behind me.

The exit to the fourth floor is barricaded with a trundle bed, two side tables and an easy chair. Everything's easy but the chair as I scrabble my way over it, rip open the porthole on its rusty hinges, and dive out – only to find myself face to face with the voice in Apartment 403.

And what a voice it is: it belongs to a statuesque dame with eyes the colour of the sky on a midsummer's day, a handkerchief of a dress, and a body in the region of thirty-nine-twenty-four-thirty-six. Most importantly, about where the thirty-nine's situated, the dame is fisting a gun – a Kirikkale MKE, to be exact, one of a truckload churned out in Turkey half a century ago, calibre either .32 or .38, depending upon your proclivities. If the signal pin tells me anything, it's that it means business.

'I've always wanted to get that door open.' The dame smiles real nice as she waves the gat at me. 'So as a little reward for your efforts, *Mr Postman*, why don't you come in? After first handing over your Smith & W, of course.'

It looks a long way from rewarding as I sidle past the Kirikkale – which is a little too much like the Walther PP as favoured by James Bond for my liking – to find myself in a mirror image of the joint I've just come from: brown carpet with more holes in it than carpet, a nice little chrome chair with a push handle and wheels on it, and wallpaper that looks like it's been clawed to death by a cat.

In the apartment below I can hear the sounds of the cops doing what cops do.

I check out the dame as she closes the door and ask the only question that's reasonable under the circumstances. 'What's with the wheelchair?'

'My father was a soldier who was involved in a number of unnecessary conflicts in the Middle East.' She's parked my Smith & Wesson but the Kirikkale stays on target. 'Unfortunately, he was shot by a fellow soldier while seated on the next bed but one cleaning a howitzer.'

They're always on the next bed but one and they're always shot by a fellow soldier.

'He was invalided home. And because no one bothered to check under the blankets, I inherited a military-issue handgun.'

I glance at the door with the frosted glass in it. 'So where is he now, this hero father of yours?'

'About where the person in the apartment below is, I expect.' She notes my raised eyebrow. 'Oh, yes,

I heard it all, only I didn't know what it was at the time – the muted conversation, a scream, the thud of what I later worked out was a body hitting the deck, the dragging of the corpse to the bed, the clatter of a knife on the sink, and the sound of someone at a computer keyboard, who shortly afterwards vacated the premises. Followed by your belated appearance.'

'Is that all?'

'Isn't that enough?'

'So why didn't you do something?'

It's the dame's turn to raise an eyebrow. 'Sweetie, where have you been all your life? Where I come from, this is the Cross. And if a person does anything more than nothing in such situations in the Cross, there's the strong possibility they'll end up like my dearly-departed war-hero father – and the victim in the apartment below.' She frowns. 'But what you haven't told me is how come you're here – a great lunk of a guy with a gun, busy pretending he's a postman. How come you turn up out of the blue, tricking your way into my neighbour's apartment?'

I want to see her reaction so I tell her. 'Because someone just killed your neighbour's boyfriend.'

'That would be Tommy Tycho.'

'How did you know it was Tycho?'

'I didn't' – cool as whisky on the rocks – 'I just knew that was the name of the boyfriend.'

So she knows that much and she also knows enough for the information not to surprise her. In the silence that follows, I hear the cops rummaging about below.

'So did you call the police?'

She shrugs. 'Do I look the sort of person who goes

around lowering property prices?'

It's an invitation to look at what sort of person she is and what I see is a dame on the high side of tall, with beautiful eyes and even nicer lips, and the sort of figure a man could create a lifetime of dreams out of. She's dressed in clothes that wouldn't look out of place on a Parisian catwalk – loose black top, a tight skirt that's no longer than it ought to be, and high-heeled clogs that accentuate her legs: the sort of totality that could raise anything on a good day, including almost the dead. Only this isn't a good day.

I'm just about to answer in the negative when there's a hammering at the door. I don't have to be Samuel L. Spade to figure who it is and that the window and a dozen sheets knotted together are my only chance of escape.

But the dame's got other ideas. She jerks the Kirikkale at the wheelchair. 'Get in!' I don't do like she tells me, so she does the logic. 'Look, Mr Postman, there happens to have been a murder and you just happen to be at – or at least unreasonably near – the scene of the crime, when you've no acceptable reason to be.' She slips my S&W into the back pocket of the chair. 'Going by what I see, even without a murder, the police will likely think you're very much a person of interest to them. You'd have to explain yourself. After that, I'd have to explain you. Which means we'd both be in all sorts of trouble. So get in.'

'Open up or we'll open up for you!'

'It's the chair or the cops, so you better do what I tell you.'

It'll never work but I do what she tells me. For one

thing there's no alternative that springs immediately to mind. For another, she's the one holding the equaliser.

'Wait!' she yells at the door. 'Now put this rug over your knees and look old.' I glance at the wig. 'Not that rug, you idiot, the blanket! The hairpiece goes on your head. All right, we're coming!'

The knocking stops and the dame's voice drops to a whisper as I hunch under the throwover like she told me to. 'Now the wig.' The rug's tresses are long and golden. The dame shrugs. 'All right, so daddy turned transvestite after he was invalided home. He was sick of pretending to be tough and so he became a girl. He told me it was his way of coping with the trauma.' She leans so close I can read the serial number on the Kirikkale. 'You know, despite pretty much everything else about you, you've got nice eyes.'

Then she parks her gat beside my S&W in the pocket of the chair and opens the door. There's a brigade waiting – enough cops to take San Quentin, sufficient blue-serge material to keep a Third World sweatshop in work for a year – dripping with walkie talkies and handcuffs and Tasers and truncheons, and fisting a glut of Glocks.

The dame wheels the chair straight at them. 'Could you bunch of unemployable cowboys get out of my way?' The fuzz hesitate. 'Look, I'll tell you this once and once only: I'm taking my mother out for some sunshine and if anyone lifts a finger to stop us, I'll sue the lot of you for the use of force in excess of requirements, got it?'

The constabulary hesitates only for a moment

before falling back. I don't know if it's the threat or the dame's cleavage that does it, but one of the two results in the door to the Otis opening, while the more able rozzers rush to assist with the chair.

'Much obliged,' she tells them, as the lift doors shut in their collective faces.

Someone must have walkie talkied the situation to the forces gathered at Ground Zero because, while we find a reception committee waiting in the foyer, instead of holding us for inquisition in their time-honoured manner, they tip their assault caps, see us onto the ramp, out into the paddock and home free.

'Where to now?' the dame asks.

I put two and two together and come up with Roarer's joint.

Chapter 5
THE FIGURE AT THE WINDOW

Rory kills people. At least that's what he used to do – before he went religious. Now he leads a peaceful coexistence in his once barely habitable hovel in Browntown, praying a lot and paving his way to Heaven with good intentions. I explain the situation to the dame while travelling in the back of one of those conveyances they custom-build to cart wheelchairs in, that look like they got their midships caught in a mangle.

Looking in his rear-vision mirror at the dame, the cabbie interupts. Cabbies always interrupt. That's why they're cabbies. 'Bloody cripples.' He stares at me perched up the back of his chariot. 'No offence, lady, but that's what she is, there's no getting away from it.' He stares at me again. 'I mean, tell me this: can you use your legs?' Break for what in some circles might pass as laughter. 'The answer's gotta be no. So we cop you. And by the time we factor in the hours spent loading and unloading your chairs and the gas these things get through, plus the possibility of getting a hernia due to all the lifting and carrying, we –'

'Shut up,' the dame tells him.

The cabbie shuts up, and it's in that condition he unloads us outside Rory's place. I chuck the wig behind the fence.

'Hey, you're not a dame and you can walk,' the cabbie says.

'And, hey,' I say, 'you just scored yourself a wheelchair.'

The joker takes off before I change my mind, leaving us to turn our attention to Rory's hovel. The falling-down fence has been replaced with nice white palings, the pathway's got shiny new pavers in it, the lawn's been given a short back and sides, and there aren't any assassins lurking in the shrubbery – at least none that I can see.

Janet, the holy-roller who latched onto Roarer after the Handless Hood caper, opens the door wearing a brown housecoat to go with the brown hair and a smile that doesn't go with anything much. The moment she claps eyes on us her smile fades to yesterday. 'Rory!' she calls over her shoulder. 'Rory, my sugar petal, come quick. He's back.'

It's a line from somewhere and I don't like lines from anywhere. Lines are inclined to have hooks in them.

'It's all right,' I tell her. 'I'm not going to ask him to do any killing. We just need a temporary refuge.'

Rory appears – still built like a greyhound and still minus one leg, and to all intents and porpoises the crutch under his armpit still doubles as a rifle. But the difference is that he's togged out in a kangaroo-shoot, and instead of the fabled killer he once was, he looks like a pacifist. The other thing he looks is at my companion.

'G'day, babe!'

Janet places a restraining hand on his crutch. 'I'm sorry, dear, but you're not meant to show familiarity towards members of the opposite sex. Under God's law, a husband shall not have any eyes left over for other women.'

I raise the brow at Rory. 'Since when did you get hitched?'

Rory shifts on his crutch. 'I didn't. Janet's being anticipatory. But, while it hasn't occurred yet, it's about to. And when it happens, I want you to be best man.'

'If it requires me to write my moniker, you're going to have to find yourself another signatory.'

'Can you give me away, then?'

'I gave you away a long time ago, pal.'

Roarer looks appealing. It takes a lot for Roarer to look appealing. 'Will you at least come to the wedding?'

'When is it?'

He checks his chronometer. 'In fifty-five minutes' time.'

'Thanks for the notice.' I shrug. 'Okay, I'll do it. But in the meantime' – I glance about – 'would you mind letting us in off the rifle range?'

My companion holds out her hand. 'I'm Monica Best. You must be Rory.'

Rory takes hold of the hand like it's a lifeline. 'Yeah, that's me, the ex-killer.' He crutches backwards into the wallpaper. 'Welcome to the reformatory.'

The joint's unrecognisable. Maybe that's what makes me nervous, or maybe it's something else, something in the innermost recesses of my mind and sideways onto my direct vision, something in the porphyry of my senses, the lurking idea we're not alone, and that somebody, somewhere, is watching us. But the boys in blue waved us goodbye at the murder scene, there was no one of interest in the vicinity, and I checked up and down Macleay Street. Plus I'd swear that no one followed the cab.

So why do I feel –

This is Browntown, so there's a mob of killers just down the road and a psychopath with a slice out of one ear contemplating mass murder by the mosque two torched hovels away, but no one looks to be after us in particular, so I shake my suspicions out of my brainpan, and lever myself into Rory's.

I don't like domestication, never have. I don't like to see Rory with his hair Brylcreemed back over his ferret skull, perched like a pimple on an anti-macassared couch, crutch-gun beside him like it's also been converted, sipping chamomile tea from a bone china teacup with his pinkie out, and smiling as though he actually *likes* people. While the dialogue follows its expected course, I let my peepers take a stroll around our immediate environs, thereby noting the following:

Christ on His Cross halfway along the salmon-pink wall; an angel with one and a half wings propped in the fake fireplace; a Bible on the table next to Rory; and a little plastic menagerie in some sort of cowshed under the window. Through which I see a figure.

'Get down!' I yell.

Rory pulls his missus onto the pretty pink carpet and somehow – he's still quick on his one foot – gets Monica down too. He's all nicely snuggled up on top of her, and I feel a pang of what might be a near-relation of jealousy as I crouch down under the *fenêtre* with my gat out, situated side-on to the drapes, while quartering the exterior. I've got the feeling – it's just a feeling – that the figure was dressed in black, or maybe it was the figure's shadow, a slim-pickings shadow with the outline of a throwing knife in its hand.

But all I can see is a neat yard with plenty of concrete and a herbaceous border around the edges and trees that look like they've been bashed into submission with a flamethrower. I can't see a knife-wielding figure – not even the shadow of a shadow of one.

I pack the gat and straighten the fedora. 'Sorry. I thought I saw something.'

Chapter 6
KILLING FOR CHRIST

Rory's back on his foot and slicking down his hair, while eyeing me like one of us is following the wrong script, and it's not him. 'I saw something, too,' he says. 'A joker that might have been in the game a caper or two too long, a palooka that's copped one punch too many, a marksman that's busy using up the few remaining bullets he's got left in his magazine shooting at shadows.'

There's an answer to that, but I don't give it. Instead I keep to the itinerary. 'No one's safe here any more, Roarer.'

He gives what in polite circles might be described as a laugh as he crutches his way back to the couch beside the Bible. '*Safe?* Pal, what would you know about safe?' He parks himself. 'Look, since I got out of killer-mode I'm as safe as anyone can get. Want to know why? Because I got God on my side, Rain. You hear me, brother? And God looks after His children, His miracles to perform.'

Which makes about as much sense as the shadow.

'Roarer, I just saw Pandora. She must have been on dog watch, waiting for me to show up.'

Roarer crosses himself. 'Like I said, Rain, I reckon you've had one spear-tackle too many, you –'

'I –'

Monica cuts across me, 'Who's Pandora?'

I owe her an explanation, so I give her the only one I got. 'Someone who's after me, a figure from my past. I don't even know what part of my past she's from, only that she wants to kill me. I also know if anyone gets in her way, she'll take them out, too.'

'But you must know . . .'

'Look, if I do know, that knowledge is buried deeper than logic in that good book of Roarer's. Meanwhile, we've got to get out of here.'

'We've also got to get to a wedding.'

Roarer and his missus-to-be exchange glances. You see this with people. Not content with exchanging bodily fluids, they also got to exchange glances.

'Roarer, if you've something to say, say it, and say it quick. Because if I know one thing about Pandora, she'll be back. And she's not about to postpone the return visit till tomorrow.'

Rory's got the crutch in one hand and the Book in the other. 'Rain, mate, I been thinking . . .'

Bad sign.

I glance out the window.

Clouds.

Otherwise nothing.

At least nothing I'm aware of.

'Anyway, we – I mean me and Janet here – well, we're all signed up to the Church of the Latter-day Hillbillies.' He looks troubled. 'Think what you like, Rain, they just happen to be the New Religion – the way, the truth and the light.' He makes it sound like an insecticide. 'Anyway, signing up means I had to give 'em my house.'

I nod. 'Smart move, Roarer.'

'That's not all.' He takes a deep breath. 'The

minister said if we wanted to be sure of getting to Heaven, we got to keep on shelling out. That means I got to find work.'

I'm starting to get the hologram, but I ask the question anyway. 'What kind of work?'

Rory does his one-shoe shuffle. 'There's only one line of employment I'm familiar with.'

'I get it: in order to get to Heaven, you got to go back to killing people?'

Rory looks uncomfortable. Then again, Rory always looks uncomfortable. Rory's an uncomfortable-looking kind of guy. 'Something like that.'

'It's not something like anything. You're either killing or you're not killing.'

He puts his foot down. 'Look, the concept's supported by the Book. *Life for life*, it says, *eye for eye, tooth for tooth, foot for foot. Exodus 28.*'

'But you've already given your foot and you've also taken out the joker that took it. What more can you do?' I glance at Janet. She's looking almost as confused as Rory's sounding. I turn back to Rory. 'Have you run this particular piece of logic past the Hillbillies?'

But if Roarer's run it past the Hillbillies, I'm not going to discover the fact this session, on account of suddenly Rory hurls his bone china teacup at the crucifix and he's down on his knee on the carpet. At first I think he's praying but then I see he's got the crutch up to one eyeball and he's loosing off a shot, followed by another and another, and on the reflex I grab Mae West in one paw and Rory's wife-to-be in the other and make for the doorway with Roarer bringing up the rear, his crutch switched to auto and still firing.

I yell to make myself heard over the fusillade. 'Where's the Caddie?'

Janet blinks behind her goggles. 'There's no Caddie any more, it belongs to the Church. We gave it to them as a down payment on the marriage, and all we could afford in its place was a 121.'

As a getaway car a Mazda 121's about as useful as a Tonka Toy. I find it hiding in the Fibrolite garage like it's just wet its pants. I shovel Rory's missus-to-be in the back and climb next to Mae West in the front, while Rory covers our rear.

And in our rear, lurking behind the shrubbery, standing so still it could be a shadow of the shrubbery, is a figure in black.

'We can't come back here in a hurry,' I tell anyone who's listening.

Chapter 7
TILL DEATH US DO PART

'Where are we headed?'

'Have you forgotten already? The leave-me-in-the-lurch, the cockies' perch, the church. Me and Janet are getting married, remember?'

'What's the hurry?'

'We were supposed to be there an hour ago.'

'I mean what's all the rush in getting hitched? She in the family way or something?'

Roarer shakes his head. 'God requires it of us.' His voice has dropped to the level of his knee. 'We're supposed to be His holy messengers, yet here we are living in mortal sin and anguish.'

The church is a church. A bunch of bricks in holy conformation, with a lot of multi-coloured windows. There's gravestones, the usual Quasimodo belltower, a garden, a parking lot, plus a not-so-usual lych-gate – corpse gate, body hatch, call it what you like – and a big bloke in a surplice ready and waiting to join two more pups asunder. We find a Holy Sepulchre and a lot of empty pews. Apart from us and the pews, there's an organ, an organ player and the preacher; you could say the ceremony might qualify as simple. I don't know what else I could expect, with Roarer the principal celebrant.

'Do you, Rory J. Smith, take Janet Q. Peters for your lawfully wedded wife?'

Rory cranes around, frowning like he's about to exx somebody. 'What did he say?'

I hunch over the gat. 'He'd like to know if you want to marry the dame.'

'Of course I want to marry the dame, that's why we're here, isn't it?'

'So tell *him* that.'

'Tell him what?'

'That you want to marry her.'

'But he already *knows* that.'

'Then tell him again.'

Roarer shakes his head and turns back to the preacher. 'Could you repeat the question?'

'Which question?'

'The one you just asked.'

'Do you, Rory Smith, take –?'

'So I can understand it.'

The preacher shrugs. 'Do you want to marry the dame?'

'That's why I'm –'

'So *I* can understand it.'

'Yeah, I do.'

'That's all I need to know.'

Janet's much quicker off the mark than Roarer – although that's never going to be the speed of a slug out of a Smith & Wesson – and before you can say *Sorry-pal-I-just-changed-my-mind-and-want-out*, Rory and Janet are hubby and missus. The organ grinder's all worked up over the Wedding Goosestep – the one by Mendelssohn, not the Wagner – and the chords are banging up into the upended-boat-frame ceiling of the holy house and dribbling down over the turn-turtle deck beams. Monica Best does signing duty in the sentencing book, and Roarer makes his mark with an X.

The preacher consults his barometer. 'If you leave now you'll still be in credit.'

Back in the bubble car, Janet asks, 'Where are we going if we can't go home?'

All I did was answer a distress call. Now I got Monica and Roarer and his missus, not to mention a debt of obligation to Annabel, which means tracking down whoever killed her – who may or may not also be the joker that took out Tommy Tycho.

'We got to get ourselves to a safe place. And on the way we got to swing by Castanet Close and pick up Imogene.'

Monica pricks up her fears. 'Who's Imogene?'

'My daughter.'

'I didn't know you were married.'

Am I imagining disappointment? 'I'm not. Me and the mother of my daughter might have parted company, but that doesn't make me divorced from the kid.'

'Why have we got to get her?'

'Because Pandora's next move – now that Roarer's joint is blown – will be to try and grab Imogene. I don't want the kid to be there when Pandora arrives.'

'But what can she do, this Pandora woman?'

I don't tell her. Just knowing is bad enough.

The little villa I bequeathed to Salina in Castanet Close is crammed between another couple of shanties of a similar ilk. The silhouette of the black-cat mobile I made Imogene still hangs in her bedroom window. Nosy Nora the neighbour is also hanging – over the side fence and hard up alongside the roller-coaster pathway to the front door.

'They're not here,' she says.

'So where are they?'

A look of smug satisfaction crosses her face. 'Forgotten already, Mr Scutt? They've gone to the kid's ballet lessons, where do you think? They never miss a Saturday. And that's what I told her.'

'Told who?'

It's Nosy Nora's moment. 'Your wife's friend, of course, the one that called by just before you did, her old schoolfriend. I said that your ex-wife and your daughter were at the Dance Academy off William, that's what I told Salina's friend.'

The only trouble with that story is that Salina doesn't have any friends.

'Was the friend wearing black?'

'I thought you said you were interested in the kid. Now you –'

'Tell me, Nora.'

Nora shrugs. 'If it was any more black, I would of said it was mourning.'

Chapter 8
THE SECRETS BOX

It's still a nice day but the clouds over the rooftops of the hovels have suddenly got greyer, and the starlings fluttering around us have turned into crows.

I call Salina on dead-man's mobile No. 3.

'Who is it?'

I've taught Salina to be suspicious. Correction: Proximity to me has made Salina suspicious.

'Seamus Devine. We met on Facebook, remember?'

Pandora's not above tapping phonecalls. Come to think of it, in this day and age no one's above tapping phonecalls.

'Oh, it's you.'

I can hear the familiar tinkle of a piano in the background, and the *shuffle-shuffle-shuffle* of tiny feet on dusty floorboards.

'Yeah.' I choose my words real careful. 'Looks like we require a termination.'

Shuffle-shuffle-shuffle. The piano's playing the black swan piece from Tchaikovsky.

'I thought everything was all right now.'

I take the breath. 'Yeah, I did, too, but I was wrong. A shadow's been discovered. So like I said, we require a termination.'

'Like now?'

'Like yesterday.'

There's a pause in which I can see the black swan leaping into the lake on her date with destiny. Then, wearily, 'Okay. Where?'

'The usual place,' I say and hang up.

I climb back into the conveyance. 'Souza's,' I tell Supergirl.

Souza's is an ice-cream parlour and it's my and Salina's emergency rendezvous of the month. Next month's Terpsichore's. It goes alphabetical.

I find Imogene wrapping her laughing gear around a blood-red imitation-strawberry double bunger, while Salina looks like she's sucking a lemon. I do the headcount.

'Where are the twins?'

I thought I had a couple of other kids – Scarlet and Rhett – until I learned they'd been fathered by somebody else, since deceased.

Salina shrugs. 'After Clint copped it, the in-laws took them away. They said I was unfit to be a mother. And it's all your fault.' Everything's my fault, even when it isn't. 'You know, I really thought when we got divorced I'd be shot of you.'

'No one's ever shot of anyone in this world, Sal.'

She steadies herself. 'So what's the score?'

'Pandora's out to kill someone.'

'How do you know it's us?'

'It's always us.'

'So where are we going?'

'I told you, the safe house.'

'That flea pit!'

Years ago, I rescued an old biddy from the clutches of a murderer. Out of gratitude, and because I wouldn't take payment, she bequeathed me an island

– or at least a shack on one. When I told her I didn't
do shacks – or any other possessions, for that matter
– by a complicated series of manoeuvres, masked
by a shelf company in the Bahamas and dead-men's
masquerades, she made the joint over to a trust fund
that could never be traced to anyone, least of all me.
It's no Taj Mahal, hence Salina's reference to flea
pits.

'Shit, Rainbow. I suppose a flea pit's better than
death.' She shoots a look at the Tonka Toy. 'But one
thing's for certain, we're not going in *that*.'

My turn to shrug. 'Sal, you got no choice. You
don't have to worry about the overload because two
of us are going pedestrian.' I nod to Supergirl, who
gets out of the Tonka Toy. 'Meanwhile, Roarer will
see you safe to your destination.'

Imogene ditches the cone. 'Can I come with you,
Daddy?'

Imogene's seven, or maybe eleven, and she likes
ice-cream. As a result she's a bit on the heavy side for
a ballerina, but that doesn't stop me thinking it's no
more than puppy fat, and one day she'll grow up to
be a nicely-proportioned mastiff.

'Not today,' I tell her. 'Today you're escaping from
the wicked stepmother.'

'Can you get my secrets box, then?'

'What secrets box?'

Imogene tells me what secrets box and where to
find it and I park the information in my memory,
alongside the image of Pandora.

'You lead an interesting life, Mr Scutt,' Monica
says as we watch them drive away. 'Or maybe I
should say Seamus Devine.'

That's when I should have got suspicious of her. But instead, all I do is shake my dumb head and say, 'It's neither.'

'All right, Mr Neether, what are we supposed to do now?'

Chapter 9
THE ROMANCE OF
THE PRIVATE EYE

I was brought up to not trust people. Trust people and one day you'll find yourself chained to a piece of masonry with reinforcement sticking out of its corrugated sides, lying among the mud crabs and turtle soup and assorted body parts and the rest of Sydney's dirty little secrets at the bottom of what's laughingly known as this burg's safe and sparkling playground. But Monica Best is a beautiful dame, and rules go out the *fenêtre* where beautiful dames are concerned.

Accordingly, after we swing by Castanet Close to pick up Imogene's box of tricks, we find ourselves at Maestro's, a classy little *nouvelle* eatery back at the Cross, my fedora on the table beside me, discussing a murder. That is, *nearly* discussing a murder.

'Before we go any further,' Monica says, 'I need to know a little more about you, Mr Postman.'

That's when she sits back, and when she sits back I notice a whole lot more about her than when she sits forward, and I don't know if that's good or bad, because the more I see of this dame, the more I want to see of her, but the more I see of her the harder it is to keep my mind on the stated objective.

'You see,' she goes on, 'all I know is that you

happened to turn up at the scene of a crime at my block of apartments. I don't even know your real *name*, or even if you possess one.'

A waiter with tattoos goes on the hover. I order a pie and Monica orders everything. I decide to come clean, or as clean as anyone can when they're dirtier than they ought to be.

'Okay, I'm a PI – that's private detective in everyday expletives – but I don't blazon my name from the rooftops because the word *private* is part of the job description. Your turn.'

'Very well, Mr Smith. I'm the original can-can girl, unfortunately born in the wrong era. Daddy went to war leaving me to make my own way, only to find that my way wasn't everyone else's and by the time he came home an invalid, I was twenty-five, and no further ahead than when he left. After that, we moved into the apartment together, shortly after which, he carked it.'

There's something Monica Best is not telling me. But, like the food in this joint, telling or not telling is not what we're here for.

'Okay, I need to know what you noticed this morning.' I take a bite out of the pie; it tastes expensive. 'Exactly what did you hear and when did you hear it?'

Monica shrugs. 'I slept late. In fact, I was still in bed when Annabel came home.'

I glance up from the pie. 'So you knew her?'

She puts down her fork. 'You said *knew* . . .'

'That's because Annabel happens to be in the past tense. But I thought you already knew that.'

'*Knowing* is different from being told. Until you

said she was dead I could pretend she wasn't.' She knuckles her eyes and takes a deep breath. 'I'm sorry, of course I know – I'm sorry, *knew* – Annabel. She was one of those beautiful people who will help anyone – a dog that's been hit by a car, a sick child, a crook. If anyone needed help, Annabel was there.'

I dole too much ketchup on the expensive *patisserie.* 'So tell me again what you heard the morning of the murder.'

Old buildings have funny acoustics, she tells me, particularly ones like hers, with wooden floors instead of concrete. And in this particular building, if you knew what you were listening for, you could hear just about everything. Monica had been Annabel's neighbour for long enough to recognise the sound of her key in the lock, and because the apartment below has the same floorplan as her own, she could also trace her movements after she entered.

Annabel went into the kitchen.

'Not the bedroom?'

'I told you, I know Annabel's apartment like it was my own. She went into the kitchen and five minutes later someone else came to the door.'

'Which door?'

'First to the door outside, the one at street level where all the buttons are, then Annabel's.'

'After she buzzed in whoever it was?'

'She didn't buzz anyone in. I told you, he came to her door.'

'How did you know it was a *he*?'

'Oh all right, it could have been a woman. After that came the scream.'

'And you didn't do anything about it?'

'Mr Smith, as I've already said, Macleay Street might be Potts Point for postal purposes, but whatever the euphemism, it's still the Cross. And in the Cross, you don't go *towards* a scream, you go *away* from it.'

'Even if it belonged to your beloved Annabel?'

'There were always screams from my beloved Annabel.'

'But you didn't think this particular scream might be different?'

For a second I have her attention. That's the romance of the private eye. It holds good right up to the moment you start asking too many questions. After that, it doesn't hold good any more.

'A third party doesn't present their credentials to women like Annabel every time they scream.' She stands on her tippy-toes. 'And if it was only sex she was screaming for, that's an even better reason not to drop in with a big smile on your face and a calling card. As I told you before, there was the scream, then typing, and after that the departure.'

I don't know where I went wrong. If I did, I wouldn't have gone there.

After Monica hits the high seas and the waiter with all the drawings on him delivers the pudding, I've got no choice but to drag out the list I culled from Annabel's printer, spread it out on the tablecloth, and eat what's before me.

Chapter 10
NOBODY LIKES A CORPSE

From what Monica told me, the list is most likely a trap. But it's something, and right now something is what I'm most in need of. There are a lot of names.

Errol 'The Pig' Shadie.

Brutus Kariakis.

Percy Smith.

Richard Presto . . .

There's more of the same but while I'm working my way through the list I become conscious of an audience, and this audience has got a scent to it, and if you asked me to put a name to the scent, I'd call it *Too Nosy For Its Own Good*. I chose this eatery because it's near where Tommy Tycho copped it, but also because it's got cloths on the tables and I wanted to impress. I thought no one would recognise me here, on account of the tablecloths.

Wrong.

I put the eating on hold and roll to the ground. At the last moment I turn the roll into a double-twist so that by the time I'm back on my trotters I'm standing behind whoever it was at my elbow. I've got my gat in the space between his fifth and sixth ribs – or between the fifth and eighth dorsal vertebrae, however you want to play it – at about the place where life starts its lonely little journey to the mortuary.

Move the right way and no one notices anything but a little more action than usual in the dining room, and by the time they think of checking the details, all they see is the waiter turning an ashen shade of jaundice, with a nattily-dressed customer standing behind and slightly to the left of him, giving him a pointer.

'And my pointer is to not look over people's shoulders.' I prod him to drive the pointer home. 'Now I'm going to pass the maître d' a C-note and tell him to keep the change while you are going to accompany me outside to give me much-needed directions to my destination, because I'm a stranger in town.'

No one looks our way. This is the Cross.

'We'll start with a name.' I've got my hat and it's back where it likes to be and we're outside the café, all cuddled up to a telegraph pole, me and the waiter and the gat. 'And after the name we'll progress to the whys and the wherefores of your curiosity.'

'I wasn't up to anything, honest!'

'Funny kind of name.'

He takes the kind of breath that tells me he wants to keep living. 'It's John.'

'Okay, Johnny-boy. Now how about telling me what your game is.'

It's a fine day. Maybe that's why he decides to tell the truth. It's nice to go on living on a fine day.

'I got a habit.'

'That'd be the habit of looking over people's shoulders that you shouldn't look over.'

'No, a *habit* habit.'

'You mean you're a junkie.'

The kid's as thin as a hangman's rope and his eyes are a day-old corpse's. 'You had a list and I saw Bro's name, so I thought –'

'You mean Mr Presto's?'

'Yeah.' The dead eyes refocus. 'I mean, yes, sir, that's what I mean. And it so happened I needed a – need a –'

'What you're saying is you need a fix and you thought I looked like a pusher. In addition to which I possessed a piece of paper with Brother Presto's name on it.'

'Yes, sir.'

I give him a prod with the gat. 'So what's with all the tatts? They make you feel big or something? Or maybe you get paid by someone to make you a walking advertisement for dragons.'

He shakes his head. 'Mates with a tattooist.'

I know what being mates with someone means. I put away the gat. I must be getting edgy in my old age. Pandora makes me that that way and jokers looking over my shoulder make me even more so.

'All right,' I say. 'See you round. And when I do, we never met, know what I'm saying?'

'Y-Yes, sir. I mean I can hear the words, but I can't even see who's saying them.'

Back on the boat next morning I get the heebies. Heebies are the creatures that visit when you're least expecting them – grey, shapeless little metro-gnomes that don't go away when you tell them to and are impervious to anything but the passage of time. It's like the whole of my back story creeps up on me and whacks me over the head with its sordid little details – the parents, the kids who bullied me at school, the failed relationships, Pandora and the rest of the jokers who are out to get me. Especially the jokers who are out to get me. Makes me understand how Tommy Tycho must have felt.

I park Imogene's tin box on the bunk she generally occupies because she'll be occupying it again, and slop into the dinghy bobbing in the Bay of Plenty. I don't have to do what I'm doing, no one's forcing me, and there's no Croesus-rich client running around waving fistfuls of moolah. So why am I doing it?

Harry Hopman's Hoop-la Parlour's open and I ask him for a caffeine hit. While I'm waiting for the muck to arrive I rescue a copy of *The Daily Terrorgraph* from the garbage bin where it belongs and smooth it open to the inside spread.

DEATH OF A LADIES MAN

No apostrophe, and no apologies for the omission. Big fat, black capitals, leaving just enough room for the cropped pictorial accompaniment – a headless body sprawled in the gutter, together with a story in the sort of prose that – if it wasn't for the subject matter – might be described as deathless:

> There are those who say he had it coming.
> Tommy Tycho, whose body was discovered yes-
> terday sprawled headless and friendless in a
> Kings Cross gutter, might have been a ladies

man – but that didn't make him anyone else's.
Tycho's death was what any respectable, law-abid-
ing Australian might describe as inevitable. Because
the whole of Sydney's underworld was gunning for
Tycho. Police say that because of this, the task of
finding Tycho's killer is a more than daunting one.
In the words of Chief Inspector Janus Leytton, head
of Operation John the Baptist, speaking exclu-
sively to the *Terrorgraph*: 'Where do we start?'
Leytton shrugs a set of shoulders that have wit-
nessed more crime than Tycho possessed enemies.
'After all, every criminal and his dog were
after Tycho. It'd be easier to begin with a
list of people who liked him and go from
there. But that would be a short list and co-
prise pretty much nothing but women.
'Because Tycho was a ladies man. What I'm saying is
there are too many suspects for us to be confident of
finding the killer inside anything under a century.'

Chapter 11
A CASE OF THE HEEBIES

While Tycho's death takes up most of the *Terrorgraph*'s first eleven pages, the other news of the day almost didn't occur. Like the two sentences on the disappearance of a backpacker in mysterious circumstances, or this little paragraph in a black-girdled box buried on page 17:

> The body of a young woman, Annabel Franklin, was discovered yesterday in her Potts Point apartment. No one was seen coming or going from the apartment but police are treating the death as suspicious. Any person or persons with information are requested to contact Kings Cross Police . . .

Straight out of the fuzz's PR file. The only thing that particular story tells anyone is that the cops are running dead on Annabel's demise, the same way they're running on the death of Tommy Tycho.

I'm just starting on another story headed *DUMMY RUN*, about a bunch of mannequins pinched from a window display in Myers department store, when someone says, 'So what do you know, Rainbow?'

I like Hopman. He's the sort of joker that looks like he's guilty of everything, yet is as innocent as an uncut lamb – old clothes, face with more lines in it than the Redfern railway terminus, and eyes a thousand times sadder than a basset's.

'Too much and still not enough.' I lean back so Harry can deposit the mugful of slop described on his menu as coffee. 'I'm trying to work out if a guy's got a duty to the dead.'

Harry pulls out a chair and parks himself. His café operates out of an old garage in an expensive residential area and rush hour is six to seven in the am when the tradies start. After that it's chat time. Harry doesn't mind. He's a philosopher.

'Said guy being you, I take it?' he says.

'That's the one.'

He shrugs and I get the profile – hunched shoulders, beak nose stuck out like a bird's bill, and mouth down at the corners like a speed bump. 'Rainbow, mate, who else have people got a duty to, if not to the dead? If you do a favour for the living it's like you expect the favour to be returned.' His chin sinks into his shirt. 'And that makes it no favour at all. In fact, it's little more than the usual quid pro quo of life.' He glances across at me out of his sad eyes. 'So what's the story?'

I tell him the story of how Annabel Franklin saved my life.

'And she killed this Pandora character?' he says.

I shake my head and it feels like it's got feathers in it. No one kills Pandora, I tell him; it's always the other way round.

'Annabel turns out the lights. Literally. She reaches up and squashes the bulb over her head with her bare hand. Then she grabs me with the hand that hasn't been shredded and drags me to safety.'

'Was she naked from the waist down?'

I do the frown. 'Harry, I'm serious. This really

happened and, no, for the record she wasn't naked from the waist down, or up, or sideways, or any other way. This event really occurred. I never clapped eyes on her before and yet that's what she did.'

'And what happened to Pandora?'

'She wings it.' I take a slurp of the slush. 'Chucks a knife that misses me by a fly's dick, then buggers off like a bat out of Lourdes. She's a one-hit girl, Pandora, and if that one hit fails, she makes herself scarce until next time.'

'You think there'll be a next time?'

I feel the heebies coming back. 'Like death follows life, Harry. Where Pandora's concerned there's always a next time.'

Harry sinks lower in his chair, looking more like a hawk than ever. Hawks are gentle creatures, in my opinion. They look bad, but are only dangerous to lambs.

'So what happens then?'

I tell him about the phone call, the headless corpse, Annabel's murder, and the dame called Monica.

'So I take it that, by some nefarious means or other, this Annabel dame finds herself dead because she phoned you regarding a potential murder.'

A black dog drifts by. Harry throws it a bit of bacon.

'That's it.'

Harry nods. 'Then I reckon you owe her one, all right, Rainbow. And I reckon you reckon the same as me. Meantime, what about this Monica?'

'What about her?'

'She could die, too, couldn't she?'

After I leave Harry's, I go straight to Mae West's, ringing her bell in the only way, et cetera and et cetera. 'It's me,' I say.

'What do you want now?' The voice is as cold as a refrigerated tomato.

'I want to apologise.'

'Because you need me?'

No. Because she needs my protection. But always tell 'em what they want to hear. 'That's only part of it.'

Monica lets me into the building and this time I take the elevator up to 403. The joint's the same as it always was. All that's missing is the wig and the chair and the happy greeting.

'What do you want?'

'Look, I figure I might have compromised you. In other words, you're in danger and I don't want another death in my overnight bag, particularly yours. I want you to join the rest of the entourage in the safe house until this is over.'

She thinks about it for a while and finally she shrugs and tells me *Yes*, in the only way, et cetera and et cetera.

But why do I sense that convincing her was too easy?

Chapter 12
THE WIDOW'S PIQUE

When a list of suspects comes your way out of the deep-blue azure during a murder investigation, there's two explanations – it's a trap or it's a trap. Accordingly, the first thing I do is pay a visit to a name that's *not* on the list, and that's the widow.

The background to Tommy Tycho is well known, but that doesn't mean I don't replay it in the back of the 399 omnibus on the way to the widow's. Tommy was a bastard. There's two ways of reading that, and you're welcome to both of them. His mother was a pro – and that doesn't mean she played tennis – while his father was a pole-punter, prepared to pay the requisite L-note for the privilege of spending seven minutes and thirty seconds with Tycho's mother-to-be with her clothes off, all of thirty-five years ago. Some 270 days later, give or take whatever there is to give or take in these situations, little Tycho was spat out into an unsuspecting world.

And as it happened, he grew up to be a good-looking bastard. An educated good-looking bastard, too – on account of after he was abandoned by his mother, he was taken in by a bunch of Cistercian monks who taught him the classics: like how to shoot people in the foot and get away with it, as well as your basic Latin. Didn't do him much good – the looks or the Latin. Tommy came out of it figuring only one thing – and that was that the world owed him a living. Call it the Adonis Complex.

There are a lot of Mr Bigs in this town and every one has got their own calling card. The cards come in the form of hobbies you'd rather not know about, or mansions dripping with CC-TVs and watchdogs as big as panthers. Or it could just be the way they walk – a swagger like they got the world between their legs, and their sole purpose in life is to keep it there. But while there are a lot of Mr Bigs in Sydney, Tycho wasn't one of them. Tycho was a dough boy. In the free enterprise world of corruption, he found a nice little niche market in parasitism. On the underside of that mongrel known as White Collar Criminality, Tycho was an active and well-fed flea.

He lived on crime, but he was never really part of it. He fed off crooks, but never dined at the same table as them. And he prided himself on never getting done by the cops for anything – not twice, not once, not ever. Tommy not only lived off the Mr Bigs of this world – robbing them, blackmailing them and sleeping with their women – he wasn't above ripping off the little man, too: the shyster, the sharper and the spiv. As a result, he had more enemies in Sydney's underworld than your average contract killer has stiffs.

He had a girlfriend.

Let's call her Annabel.

He also had a wife.

Let's call her the widow.

I find the widow in a falling-down joint in Maroubra, just around the corner from a play gym, a Dulux paint parlour and a *patisserie.* It's the kind of hovel you wouldn't park a dog in – if you had any respect for the dog – with a fence that if it leant any more would be firewood, weeds sticking up from mashed-potato concrete like hair out of the skull of a leper, and walls that need another coat of paint, if for no other reason than to keep them upright.

There's a stench about most things these days, but the smell coming out of this joint is the sort on which a dead dog could be successfully grafted, the kind of smell that if it was at a mausoleum you'd say it was where it belonged, a stink that if it was on your leg you'd have the offending member amputated, if only to ensure the gangrene didn't spread any further.

Crooks have got dolls and they got molls, but going by the face on the dame that raises the portcullis, Angela Tycho is neither. The story goes that when some thug threatened to exx her on account of a stunt Tycho pulled, he just laughed and said go ahead and do it. It might have been a bluff or maybe it wasn't, but whatever it was, it worked.

Angela's face mightn't have been her fortune, but at least she didn't die from it. Her looks were her insurance then and still her insurance now, a little grey-haired potoroo wearing a torn plastic apron without any frills and a troubled look on her homely features that descends all the way to the dangle-down stockings around her ankles.

'Would you be from the police?'

I peer into a lounge room that's coloured

puce-pink like the rest of the joint, with a view through the window of next door's toilet, and find that the smell just got that much stronger.

I wave away a fly. 'Yeah, the police is exactly where I'm from.'

She nods. 'I was wondering about your taking so long, particularly after handing him over. I expect you'd like to know where I was when my husband died.'

'I'm sorry, but it's just something we got to do, Mrs Tycho.'

'My real name's Tychopoulos – Angie Tychopoulos. Tommy had the name altered to further his career.'

'And what career might that have been?'

She looks surprised. 'Why, public relations, of course.' She seems to believe it, but that doesn't mean I got to. 'He did good works for people, a lot of it on a *pro bono* basis.' She glances at me. 'That means for nothing.'

I don't tell her I already know what it means. I'm supposed to be a cop and a cop wouldn't know *pro bono* from a professional pop singer.

'You see, my Tommy was more of a public benefactor than people gave him credit for. He was so good it was difficult to know how he ever made a living. But that was just one of the many reasons I had for loving him.'

She's trying to establish her love for her husband as an alibi, only it doesn't work that way.

'Look, Mrs Tycho, ma'am – I'm sorry, Tychopoulos – no one's saying you did anything.'

She clasps her hands and leans forward like she's

doing callisthenics. 'That's right, because why would I kill Tommy?' Tears come to her eyes. 'Oh, he was so good to me, Tommy was, you wouldn't believe it. His life was such a struggle, one way or another, due to his unfortunate beginnings. But he always put first things first, and the first thing Tommy did was set me up in this lovely little home and see to all my needs.'

Second alibi: No grudges. But it still doesn't work that way.

She waves a skinny paw at her stinking surroundings. 'Oh, I know it isn't much to look at, but it's as good as Tommy could manage, given all his setbacks.'

If the joint was nicer than it is, I'd still say the widow lived in fairyland. But there are worse places than fairyland and if she wants to live there, she's welcome to it. Only I'm not after fairies, I'm after the troll that killed Annabel Franklin.

'And what setbacks might they be, apart from his beginnings?'

'All those people who for reasons best known to themselves, didn't –' She pauses. 'Look, I don't know if you're aware of it, Mr –'

'Smith, Detective Inspector Bert Smith. But just call me Inspector.'

'I'm sorry, Inspector. As I was saying, a lot of people seemed not to have liked my Tommy, for reasons best known to themselves. I never understood why, unless it was simply because he was too good – too good for his own good, really.' She shakes her head. 'People have never taken to saints, at least, not while they're alive. Look at Joan of Arc.

I believe Tommy's very goodness made other people
feel bad in comparison, so they hated him for it.'

Chapter 13
THE CORPSE IN THE KITCHEN

I take notes. Only it's hard to focus on anything given the smell. 'And what else do you know, Mrs Tycho – sorry, Tychopoulos?'

'That Tommy would have been a great man if he'd lived.'

I write: *Delusional*. Then I stare through the smell at the Widow. 'Only he didn't live, did he?'

She takes a deep breath, which is more than I dare do. 'He trusted people too much, Tommy did.' She stands. 'But, oh dear, I didn't offer you a cup of tea. What on earth would Tommy say?'

A lot more than he can now he's dead. I put the sort of expression on my dial-up that might be appropriate to the occasion. 'Look, Mrs – T – I didn't come here for cookies, as I'd say you got enough on your plate without adding biscuits. All I need to know is where you were on the morning in question. After that, I can get the hell out – I mean, leave you alone.'

She aims for a smile but misses and it comes out a grimace. 'Oh, that's easy. It's like asking someone where they were when Oprah announced her weight loss or Lady Di told the world she'd been unfaithful to Prince Charles or they found Fergie sucking that horrible man's toes in her swimming costume. On the morning in question, I was at the butcher's buying scotch fillet for Tommy because he was coming home. I hadn't been to the butcher's for, oh, for ages, because meat's so expensive. I'm sure Mr Simms would remember my being there.'

I write: *Query meatmonger.* Then, 'One more question.' There's always one more question, even when there isn't. 'Given that it wasn't you that did the job on your late and much-lamented husband, who would you say killed him?'

She shakes her head. 'As I said, he had so many enemies . . .'

I get to my feet. I've got my nosewipe out and I'm clutching it to the *schnozz.* 'Well, thank you Mrs –' I've got to put the question – the smell's an elephant in the room and the place is humming with flies. 'Can you tell me: is there something dead around here?'

The dame smiles. It's the first real smile she's thrown me since I been in the joint, a glow like the dawn over distant hills, stars through clouds, the glimmer of what might have been but never can be, on account of a miserable little, tricksy-dicksy, cheating loverboy by the name of Tommy Tycho.

'Why, yes, as a matter of fact there is, Inspector. I'm sorry I didn't show you before but I thought as a policeman you'd already know.'

Show me what? Know what? I recall what she said about the cops handing something over as I follow her through a doorway squashed between a migration of bright-green plaster ducks lining the walls and along a hallway, where I pause long enough to get a lungful of life-giving air while helping myself to a piece of paper I find lying on the floor by the telephone. Then I move on. And all the while the smell's getting stronger and the flies more numerous, until I know I'm going to find myself in a cesspit, or dead from putrefaction, or both.

Just before the final doorway, I stop. Even I've got my limits. 'Look, Mrs Tychopoulos . . .'

The smile's still there – if anything, it's even brighter – and one outstretched arm's pointing at something hidden from me. 'No, *you* look, Inspector.'

So I take one more fateful pace that gets me to the doorway that leads to the kitchen, and what I see is something I've never seen before and never want to see again, even if it kills me. And that's a green kitchen chair in the middle of the floor, and seated in the chair like it belongs there, a corpse with a ring-a-ring-a-rosy of words in a necklace around its neck – which just happens to be headless.

I reel back, as much on account of the sight as because of the smell. 'Jee-sus!' I say to no one in particular. 'It's Tycho!'

'Of course it's Tommy!' The widow's picked up a can of Mortein and is busy applying a liberal dose to the hole in the corpse's neck. All it does is excite the flies. 'Who did you inspect it to be, Expector? I mean . . .'

But I know what she means, and what she means is: how come I don't know – if I'm from the rozzers like I say I am – that the widow was granted custody of her dead husband's body prior to burial, because:

1. The cause of death was as obvious as the nose on other people's faces.

2. No ID was necessary because of the tattoo around the neck.

3. The cops no longer required the stiff because

they were running dead on the death of Tommy
Tycho: they were otherwise employed and besides,
he'd had it coming.

I still ask the question. 'What's he doing *here*?'

The dame shrugs. 'I believe in reincarnation.
That's why he's here and –'

But I'm not hanging around for explanations.
I head back to where I can breathe, drag open the
front hatchway and stay alive. 'Look, I know what
reincarnation means, but how come they palmed
you the corpse?'

She shrugs. 'I just asked and the police seemed
relieved to be rid of him. They said that the cause of
death was obvious and that Tommy was just taking
up space. They even bent him into a sitting position
for me.'

'What about their inquiries?'

She throws me a sweet expression. 'Don't you
mean *your* inquiries, Inspector?' She doesn't wait
for an answer. 'Tommy will be here for three
days.' She nods fondly to herself. 'Three days,
after which comes the funeral.' She smiles. 'It's
winter, so decomposition isn't as quick as it might
be.' She takes a deep breath; it's nice that someone
can. 'Meanwhile, I'm trying to find somebody to
bury him. Everybody says there'll be trouble but
why should there be trouble at a funeral? Do you
happen to know of anyone who would bury Tommy,
Inspector?'

I don't and I change the subject. 'I found a piece of
paper in the hallway with a lot of stuff crossed out,
leaving nothing but the word *Orange*.'

The dame's face goes mottled. 'Did you?'

'Yeah, I did.' I take the papyrus out of my skyrocket and uncrumple it. 'Look.' I prod at all the cross-outs that obliterate most of the writing, then at the only word left legible, the one at the bottom. 'See how it says *Orange*? Now I got to ask myself: why would a piece of paper be lying around with the word *Orange* on it?'

Her brow creases. 'What else have you helped yourself to, Inspector?' The brow uncreases, and the voice becomes the widow's again. 'Oh dear, I'm terribly sorry if I seemed rude just then but please understand I've just lost my husband. I know that's no excuse for throwing wild accusations around, and after all you are from the police.' She nods, as if to herself. 'But I remember now.' She glances around her. 'You see, I won't be able to stay here now that Tommy's gone. Because of his altruism, I'm broke. I'm going to have to sell up everything to survive. And of course I'm having the house painted and the colour I'm going to have it painted is –'

'Orange.'

It figures. Flea-puce to orange. I put on the fedora together with my just-born-yesterday look, the one with all the innocence in it. 'From memory, at the time of Tommy's demise you say you were at the baker's?'

She shakes her head. 'No, it was the butcher's. Mr Simms's, to be exact, on Anzac Parade.'

Chapter 14
THE CRONE IN THE QUEUE

Unlikely as it is that Tommy's widow could ever have toted an elephant-gun – much less fired it without incurring more damage to herself than to the corpse – you're not much good in this game if you place your faith in the unlikely. As a result, the next step in the *pas-de-dur The Death of a Ladies' Man* (note the apostrophe), is to check out the alibi she palmed me. When I do this, I discover the butcher's got blood on his hands. His mitts are dripping with the stuff but he wipes off the gore like it's no more than an afterthought, all the while eyeing me like I'm just another sausage, and therefore part of the food chain.

'Who'd you say you was?'

'I'm an inspector of police.'

He nods his butcher's head. 'Yeah, and I'm second cousin twice-removed of the Mona Lisa.' Simms places his fists on his display case and leans over them. 'Why don't you tell me what you want me to believe you want to know and I'll decide if I want to let you know it?'

I ignore the implications and read from my notebook like it's some kind of official document. 'I'm inquiring into the death of Tommy Tychopoulos, specifically, the whereabouts of his wife Angela on the morning in question.'

The butcher shakes his head and tries out a laugh that would look good on an orangutan. 'What, that little thing? Mate, if you reckon she had anything to do with it then you lot must be an even greater bunch of mugs than the newspapers say you are. Sure, Tycho was bad to the bone, but Angie's the last person who'd duff him.'

'We still need to verify where she was on the morning in question. She says she was here.'

'That'd be yesterday. Yeah, she was here all right. For going on an hour she was here, if you really want to know.'

I tell him, yeah, I really want to know.

'Look, Angie's the kind of shiela who's always at the end of the queue. There must have been twenty customers come into my shop after she did and I guarantee she apologised to every one of them, before letting them in front of her. So she was here a bloody long time.'

'You sure it was her?'

Simms chucks me the sort of look than could only come from a butcher. 'As sure as I am that you're a rozzer, mate.'

There are jokers that would call me paranoid. But when you been in this game as long as I have, you got a lot to be paranoid about. Apart from which, paranoid's the kind of insurance a private eye needs – if only to keep him alive for a period slightly longer than the lifespan of your average beetle.

So when I emerge out of the flesh-vendor's onto

Anzac Parade and join the hodge-podge of animal life that calls itself humanity, I realise not only that Tommy's widow possesses a cast-iron alibi, but also that there's someone watching my every move – and as usual I pay a lot of attention to that feeling.

Anzac Parade is the kind of thoroughfare people die on. It's named after a war – the second A and the C stand for Army and Corpse respectively – and this morning it's busy living up to its name, with traffic forcing its way through the roundabout, every second punter acting like they got nothing better to do than carry a grudge against the rest of their fellow travellers, and someone following me. I'm not concerned with the punters I can see, it's the ones I can't see that I'm worried about.

I scan the buildings across the goat track, but all I see is a dame doing her nails, a cat perched outside a white-anted window pretending to be asleep, and a kid staring bleak-eyed at an unpromising future. Otherwise, there's no more than a few tattered curtains and a whole lot of darkness. But I still get the hell out of there, and while I'm doing that I ask myself the following questions: Who would know I'm here? And who would take the trouble to follow me, once they knew?

Together the questions are almost as big as how the world began, so I catch a cab to White Bay then ride the 397 back to the city. I take Shanks's pony to the Big Pond – also known as Sydney Harbour – and when I'm pretty certain I've shaken off any pursuer, I find a boat that no one's using and row to the remote inlet where I've temporarily parked the *Wooden No.* There's no place like home, even when it's a boat.

I call Rory on dead-man's mobile No. 3.

'That you Rainbow?'

I sever the connection. Most of the time Roarer's brain's on auto-pilot and most of the time the auto-pilot's suffering a serious malfunction. I dig another mobile out of the *Wooden No*'s bilge and try again.

'This – is – John – Smith.' I say it slow and deliberate. '*Smith*, got it? Smith as in packet of potato chips, the kind of dainties they hand around at the funerals of idiots whose fatal problem in life was they were terminally careless.'

There's a pause. 'Gotcha.' Another pause. 'Mr Smith, it is, then. So what can I do you for?'

I stay with the code. 'How's your family?'

Roarer stays stupid. 'Pal, you know as well as I do that I ain't got no family, apart from the new wife, and she's . . .'

I can hang up again or I can persevere. I persevere. 'Nice little homily, Mr *Daughter*.'

The usual pause. Sometimes I think Roarer's brain might have been amputated along with his leg. 'Oh, *that* family. Yeah, right, they're all good.'

'Have you had any visitors?'

'What have visitors got to do with the price of flounders?'

I think of Roarer tangling with the vicissitudes of life. One thing in his favour is he wouldn't notice most of them, they'd go over his head faster than a slug from a Steyr Bullpup.

'It's *code*,' I tell him.

'Oh, right, gotcha,' he says again. 'No, no one's bothered us. Everyone's – Look Mr – you know, Smith, or whatever you're calling yourself – can I go home?'

'You are home. For the foreseeable future, that's where you happen to be, unless you want to make a graveyard your home. Look, on second thoughts, maybe we better have a little talk.'

'When?' Roarer sounds like he's at his wits' end. It hasn't taken long. Then again, we're talking about Roarer's wits.

'Sooner rather than later.'

'What's that supposed to mean? Look, you got no idea what it's like here, it's a *jungle*. We got mosquitoes as big as cows and ticks the size of dogs and as for the fleas, Jesus wept! I swear I saw this *boa constrictor* yesterday, it was –'

I cut him off before he lets the snake out of the bag, the cat out of the closet, the whereabouts of his and Imogene's and the rest of the tribe's place of hiding to whoever might be listening, by way of association. 'Sooner rather than later' can only have one meaning. But one thing's for certain, it's not now.

Chapter 15
DEATH COMES TO THE CLEANERS

I'm outside the dry cleaner's that acts as a front for Errol 'The Pig' Shadie aka the brothel king. There's enough silence to hear the footsteps approaching, and also enough moonlight on this clear, cold night to see the flash of a knife. I roll to one side, tucking my knees up hard under me. I thrust myself into the first position before launching myself skywards, coming back down to Ground Zero as far from the blade as I can, while still keeping myself as close to upright as humanly possible.

My attacker is a small joker – long hair, loose clothes for easy movement, and dingo-headed – but still as sharp as the stiletto he's wielding. In the moonlight I can see the tension in the crouch and know that any moment he could do me, given the chance. Only I'm not giving him the chance because I don't particularly want to be done. I hurl myself onto both hands and cartwheel in the opposite direction to the one he thinks I'll be going in, namely *at* instead of *away from* him, my whitesides crunching into his portside malar, *en passant*. But he's a pro, I can tell that by the speed with which he regains his equipoise, squatting over his centre of gravity like he's been in this situation before, and shaking his head to clear a sightline skewed by the bruised cheekbone, knife gripped between thumb and forefinger in a way that tells me he's got more than a passing idea of how to use it.

It's Saturday night at the movies, and lovers are strolling arm in arm within rifle's length of us, but that's no help when you're dead, and if I don't keep my wits about me that's how I'll find myself, well before the projectionist turns up the lights at intermission.

The joker's wearing black and he's skinny and as a result an anorexic alley cat would make more of a target.

My next move could be my last.

I don't want my next move to be my last.

Accordingly, I put my next move on *Pause.*

A ship's hooter sounds in the Harbour and maybe I flinch or maybe he just expects me to, but it can't be coincidence that the instant the hooter goes off he makes his death leap, and I find him hovering above me like a fruit bat on steroids. I've got my arms out and fingers spread the way James Cagney did in – well, like a funambulist on a tightrope to nowhere – but since the hoods robbed me of my portside thumb, I'm not as balanced as I might be, and I stumble.

That's when the joker's onto me.

It's more luck than good management, but at the last nanosecond I manage to deflect the blade, hearing it rattle against my ship's anchor cufflink as I bring up the portside arm, and even in this twilight of the gods I see the look of surprise on his half-dog face, at the same instant as I catch a whiff of the animal sweat in his nearside armpit as he goes by. It's the smell that tells me I've got a chance. When a skinny joker sweats on a cold night, it means he's nervous, and when he's nervous he's acknowledging the possibility of defeat. All I've got to do is realise that possibility for him.

He's behind me, and like any experienced assassin he expects me to mimic his movements as though we're executing a death dance. But I stay the way I am, facing the window of the dry cleaner's together with the reflection of my would-be killer behind me. That reflection tells me he reckons that all he's got to do after moving is sink the knife in.

In the event, that's what he does.

They generally do plate glass shatter-proof these days. It's in all the city's building regulations. But this is the Cross, and they do things differently here. The vitreous material is very much of the temporary variety — the same variety as my would-be killer turns out to be made of. The alarm goes off and stays going off. By the illumination of the little blue gizmo above the hatchway, I can see the blood leaking from the figure lying among all the glass-spattered clothes.

Any man's death diminishes me because I am involved in Mankind. And therefore never ask for whom the bell tolls, it tolls for thee.

Or words to that effect.

I kneel and take the skinny joker's head in my hands. 'You're going to be all right.'

'No, I'm fucked. What did you have to go and move for?'

'I wanted to stay alive.'

He frowns, like he's trying to come to grips with a thought that's rapidly drifting towards the farthermost limits of its comprehension. 'What about me?' If I didn't know better I'd say there was an attempt at a smile. 'You selfish bastard.'

But there's a reason I spent too many hours outside a dry cleaner's. It's the head office for a string of brothels, and there's something I got to know. 'Did your boss kill Tommy Tycho?'

The back-to-base siren's hooting like a tawny frogmouth that hasn't had a feed since downing a native marsupial a week ago, while the blood of my would-be assassin is soaking into my hands like cordial at a children's knees-up, and I'm starting to believe I'm never going to get an answer, when suddenly I see the hood's thin little lips move.

I lean closer. 'What did you say?'

Again the smile, only I can see now that it's not really a smile at all but the sort of expression you see on the skull of a dead man, otherwise known as a rictus. 'Tycho had evidence against my boss in an underage prostitution case but my boss didn't do the job because . . .' I lean closer. '. . . someone got in before him.'

He's making a big effort and in that effort I can see his childhood and also how that childhood might have been something very much like mine had I not had my Aunt Rube. What could anyone expect other than this kid'd turn out the way he has, somebody's miserable little would-be assassin lurking in dark alleys, failing to kill innocent people for a pittance?

'So why did you try and off me?' I ask.

'You was prying, wasn't you? What did you think Pig was gunna do, send you a welcome card?'

I lay the skinny hood's head down as gentle as I can – just as a white car with a black stripe and the word SECURITY along the side noses around the corner.

Chapter 16

THE MAN THAT DIDN'T BELIEVE

They're big and they've their shaved heads and there's two of them. They've relieved me of the gat so I go quiet, or as quiet as can be expected under the circumstances, which involve them pushing me around a bit after the security turkey makes himself scarce, before dragging me in through an Orb-steel door and up two flights of stairs, where they dump me before the Pig like a truffle.

He's propping up a leather-inlay desk. If he was any smaller he could be mistaken for a babe-in-arms, except his head isn't one you'd find on any mother's bundle of joy – a phyzog like a wild boar's, with dead blowflies for eyes, a snout, and a mouth that might have been put there by a madman with delirium tremens and a lino-cutter.

'Well, if it isn't Mister Rainbow.'

Just like I know Sydney's underworld, Sydney's underworld knows me. But if there's any respect to go with the knowledge, it isn't mutual.

'Evening, Pig.'

Pig snarls. 'Before I have you properly seen to, would you mind telling me why you were snooping around?' It's a nice voice, with lots of cultured tones in it. But that doesn't make the message any sweeter.

'I have reason to believe –'

'No reason, please. And no beliefs, either.' He picks up my gat off the inlay where one of the goons dropped it along with my hat and waves it around the orifice. 'You see, this is a reason-and-belief free zone. So none of your bullshit, okay? All I want to know is why you're poking your snout where it isn't wanted.'

'You killed Tommy Tycho.'

Pig laughs. It's nice to see people laugh. Only I wouldn't categorise Pig as people. 'That creep!' He replaces my gat next to my fedora. 'Rainbow, those of us who have made a success of ourselves in this world don't have much time for the likes of pretty boys. And Tycho was a pretty boy, someone who got lucky and thought all he had to do was lie back and enjoy it. He was also a slug and I don't like slugs anywhere near my flowers.' Pig might have been referring to his goons, only I doubt it. 'But I didn't kill him. I would have liked to, but I didn't.' He frowns. 'The word around the traps, Rainbow, is that the job was done by none other than you.'

'Nice theory.' I don't call him Pig but that doesn't mean I got to call him anything else. 'Only there's such a thing as motive. You had one – I didn't. He jammed your missus – I didn't. He was providing witnesses against you in a prostitution case – I wasn't. You hated him – I didn't. I just happened to find myself at the scene of the crime.'

Pig shakes his head. 'Not crime, Rainbow – *crimes*. There were two murders that day and you happened to be at both of them.'

It's my turn to shake the head. '*After* the event. In

both cases. And again: I didn't have a motive.'

Pig leans forward, his mouth hanging open. 'Oh, but they say you did, they say you most absolutely did. Because I hear you were sweet on the girl.'

I'm being fitted for something, and it's not a new pair of Y-fronts.

'You probably think I'm playing with you in much the way a cat plays with a mouse,' Pig goes on. 'But the fact is that, while I had every reason to want Tycho dead, I was at the Dentist's on the morning in question.'

I do the frown. 'Your choppers look okay to me.'

Act stupid and people given you answers to questions you didn't even ask.

'And you call yourself a detective. De*fect*ive, more like.' Pig stares at his goons until they remember to simulate laughter. 'I was referring to my friend Karl *Laughing Gas* Petrie. That's where I was on the morning in question, with my dear friend Karl, arranging a delivery of dollies for my girls.'

The answer to the question I didn't ask.

'Okay,' I say, 'so you were obtaining drugs for underage prostitutes. That's bad but it's not murder. Why not let me put you in the clear on the death rap?'

Pig aims for an expression of disbelief, but only manages an outer. 'I don't need you or anyone else to put me in the clear. You might be a detective but you're not the cops. As far as they're concerned, whoever put Tycho away did everyone a favour. Which, as we all know, is why the police are running dead on the issue.' He glances at me out of his beady eyes. 'But would you mind telling me how you got the name Rainbow? It sounds like something you'd find in a showbag, no offence intended.'

I tell him no offence taken and also how I got the name – how my mum was a Nimbin hippy who dived into a dam when her waters broke, and when I bubbled to the surface a rainbow formed. It could have been worse: could have been an eclipse. This is all a way of stalling the inevitable until I can work out a way of avoiding it altogether.

It's the goons' turn to laugh now, and my interlocutor joins in the general merriment and the atmosphere in the designer orifice is close to festive.

This is my chance, so I take it, placing my elbows in the region where the thugs are laughing, before turning on the half-step to put myself in the appropriate position when their heads come down. I haven't got two fists for nothing, and I'm busy deploying them to good advantage when a bullet whangs past my head. I crouch down just as Pig looses off a second slug out of my Holy Terror, stepping behind him and applying a half-Nelson before relieving him of my gat as the thugs get to their feet and move forward with the clear intention of putting me in the letterbox.

I twist Pig's trotter. 'Tell them to stay where they are or I'll break your *raison d'être*.'

Pig squeals. 'Stay where you are!'

The thugs stay where they are.

I tighten the hold. 'Now listen up. You wanted me taught a lesson and I'm very much inclined to return the favour. However, not having had all the fine education you did, I won't, unless you force me to. Instead, I'm going to find out who killed Tycho.

And if it turns out to be you, I'll be back – not because I'm carrying a candle for Tycho, but because of the other death that day. Got it?'

There's no answer, so I shake his responses.

'I said, *got it?*'

'Yeah, I got it,' Pig grunts. 'Look, I haven't done anything.'

'Then tell me who did.'

Pig's still got a squeak in him. 'I don't know. But if it was anyone, it was the Dentist. Tycho took a load of bo-diddlies off him and never paid up.'

It could be true. Then again it could be a bunch of raspberries. I turn to go.

'Rainbow?'

'Yeah?'

Pig's cradling his twisted trotter. 'I believe Tycho hasn't been buried yet.'

'I thought you didn't believe anything.'

'As I said, I didn't kill him. But that doesn't mean I didn't *want* him dead. I'd like to go to his funeral, if only to pay my final disrespects.' He chucks me a look that might be described as pleading, if it was on someone else. 'So could you organise it for me?'

I tell Pig I'll keep it in mind.

Chapter 17
BREAKFAST WITH RUBE

While the dame that did me the favour of a lifetime is lying on a slab in the Glebe Mortuary – as dead as Anne Boleyn after her little set-to with Henry – Rory, his newly-wed, my daughter, her mother and a beautiful broad named Monica Best are holed-up in the safe house.

I figure it's time to pay Aunt Rube a visit. Rube's presently out of the freezer: sometimes she's in and sometimes she's out, and at the moment she's back in the home she's always had, a rundown terrace in a rundown part of East Sydney. This is where she brought me up in the only way she knew how, after Dad dumped me on her when Mum blew her lolly on the fruit farm.

I take the alternative route, past the bespoke tailor's in Oxford Street that affords me a replacement for an outfit that's become too careworn to go unnoticed in public. I go for a nice yellow shirt with pink polka-dots on the façade, a bag of fruit in pale-green linen with silver and gold flecks in it, and a yellow fedora.

Rube's still Rube, a slight figure with short-cropped hair, dressed in black, all skin and ribs when I hug her, but tough as Kraut steel when she needs to be. She's the hardest little number you'll ever come across — weight for age — this side of a kung-fu parlour in downtown Chinatown.

'You're looking well.' She glances up and down the boulevard before shutting the door. 'So what's she like?'

'She's got cornflower-blue eyes.'

I radioed ahead so Rube's already got the tomatoes, eggs and mushrooms humming on the back burner.

'*Has*, Rainbow, *has* — not *gott*. *Gott*'s German for God.' She sighs like she always does when she corrects me. 'But you always were a sucker for blue, weren't you? So, she a risk?'

I shrug as I sit. 'She can handle a gun and she can think fast.' Rube's one person that can make me see things just by asking questions. 'So, okay, I guess, all right, yeah . . .'

Rube shakes her head. 'Jesus, Rainbow, you and broads. So what else are you involved in, apart from the eyes?'

With the daylight that's flickering through the small window lighting up the Willow Pattern on the dresser, I bring her up to speed.

'So to avenge this Annabel Franklin dame,' she says after I've finished my spiel, 'you're taking on a case that's going to pay as much as an also-ran at Randwick?'

'I got to do it, Rube.'

'Of course you *have* to, Rainbow. That's how you're made.' She sighs again and looks at me thoughtfully. 'And if anyone would know how you're made, I would, wouldn't I – seeing as I made you.' She composts herself. 'Is there anything I can do?'

'As it happens, Rube, yeah, there is.' I tell her the list of phone calls, calls I'd rather my name wasn't attached to.

'That all?'

I nod. 'Unless there's something you know that I don't concerning Tommy Tycho.'

Rube shakes her head. 'Only the fact that everyone hated him – but then the whole world knows that. And also the miraculous fact that he was clean. Because they never pinned anything on him, did they – apart from the toe tag they put on him after he died.'

I polish off the caffeine. 'Yeah, quick on his feet, was our Tommy.'

'You could say that. Then again you could say he wasn't quick enough.' She looks at me over my empty mug; it's the kind of look I'm used to, the look an aunt throws you that's taken care of you since you were a babe, the sort of look you can never escape from. 'Okay, I'll do the phone calls, Rainbow. But you'll have to do me a favour in return.'

I glance at her wary. 'Depends on the favour.'

'I want you to use Rory.'

'I'm using him as much as I can. He's looking after the kid in the safe house. Apart from which, he's found God and got married.'

'Didn't you tell me he was prepared to go back to killing in order to finance his beliefs? And can't your new-found flame look after Imogene? You've already told me she can handle herself.'

My turn to do the sigh. 'Okay, Rube.' I haul myself off the stool. 'Meanwhile, I better get moving or I won't get moving at all.' Rube suddenly looks smaller than I remember. 'But what about you?'

She shrugs. 'I'm fine. The day you need to care about me, Rainbow, I'll take a one-way boat trip to the Azores.'

Chapter 18
SAFE NO MORE

It's a breezy winter's morning with seagulls dipping their orange-red ice-breakers in the spindrift as I push off past the punters at the No Peer café. I scan the phyzogs to see if there are any with latent murder in them, before parking myself low in the belly of the boat, taking hold of the tiller and setting sail in the opposite direction to the one that leads to the safe house. The tide's out and mud's in the ascendancy – greasy muck like the stuff they started the world with, a primaeval soup steaming off the shore of the bush-mangled island. I beach the skiff after going round the world to get there – and am just starting the long haul up the uneven steps into the jungle when someone starts taking pot shots at me.

I dive into the undergrowth, a tangle of blackberries, biddy bush and lantana. There's nothing natural about it, just as there's nothing normal about the gunfire. A second shot wings past my cakehole, followed by a third. The weapon's a .275 by the sound of it – and also by the sound of it, the safe house where I parked Imogene is safe no more. My heart goes into ragtime, the sort of beat Charlie Ellis was always looking for but could never find. Imogene's up there somewhere. And by the sound of the artillery, there's a good chance she'll never eat ice-cream again.

I resume the ascent, only a lot quicker this time, keeping away from the makeshift steps – instead fighting the whips and tendrils of the creepers, at the same time as I'm fighting my fears. It could be whip birds, or it might be fairies. Except that whip birds and fairies don't ricochet and bounce past your skull and leave marks on rocks in passing.

A deep, dark, cantilevered cliff blocks my path and I've got to work my way around it. That makes it slippy-slide time, with the whitesides turning to one-tones and my heart to mush. Because somewhere among all this gunfire is my daughter.

I force the panic to a minimum. The shooter's either Pandora or the killer that snuffed out Tycho and Annabel – unless it's no more than yet another random psychopath.

A direct line to the hut opens up, but I don't take it. If someone's gunning for me, that's what they'll line up their rifle on. I have to get there sooner or later, but sooner or later's not now. Accordingly, I head for the high ground, leaving the Smith & Wesson nestled in the shoulder-holster as I hand-and-knee it past the ablution block, up around the dead-logs-for-charity section and the mosh pit where pioneers mined out naked dreams in the island's innocent past.

After that, it's around the remains of the dead kangaroo and the live red belly Joe Blake that appears out of its hole in the ground, angling away from the shack so I can come down on the bullet thrower from the high ground, climbing to my feet by the big smoky gum and hightailing it into the wilderness.

I could be a brush-tailed wallaby or a kangaroo.

Then again, I could be dead.

Another bullet gets airmailed my way, followed by another.

They're onto me, which means I got to switch tactics and take the alternative route, the one that takes me via the water tank I installed when a friend of a friend of a friend – no names – first put this place my way more years ago than I care to remember, along in front of the wind-turbine and the nest of solar-plates, so I'll have the height advantage when I meet up with whoever's loosing off the musketry, as well as having Old Sol behind me, right where I want him to be.

Suddenly there's a whole lot of silence, silence in which I can contemplate the nice panorama from the top of the mountain, the ins and outs of the Hawkesbury and the toy train trundling over the centipede bridge to nowhere, experiencing a cool breeze that tells me I better do something fast, or not bother doing it at all.

Movement below at 10 o'clock.

To hell with the noise, the gunfire can only mean one thing and that is that Roarer and the dame are putting up a fight. It might be Pandora, or it might be the assassin, but two things are for certain – it's not a couple of Seventh Day Adventists spreading the good word, or the Avon Lady.

I haul out the equaliser and head south. My portside whiteside catches on a ficus root but at the last instant I manage to change the fall into a tumble. I bring up an arm, lose my equilibrium, and slam into the water tank. A shot zings into the tank.

'Come out with your hands up or you won't be coming out at all!'

I recognise the dulcets.

'Roarer!'

'Rainbow!'

'Rory, you bloody idiot! Hold your fire!'

'It's not my fire,' he yells back, 'it's the kid's. Anyway, what are you doing scaring the crap out of us?'

I shelve the gat and work my way back to reality.

They've been doing target practice – Roarer, Monica Best and Imogene. Don't worry about safe houses and forget about silence being golden, or even copper-coloured – the four of them have been busy whanging away at tin cans while Rory's dame and the ex are having a parley for two in the cowshed.

I herd the shooters back to the chateau.

'Did you bring my box, Daddy?'

I can't remember everything. 'Sorry, kid, I left it on the boat.'

The kid takes the information in her stride. 'Roarer says I'm shooting real good.'

'*Well*,' I tell her.

I sense the dame striding beside me stiffen.

'Is that all you can say – *Well*? Imogene's been so pleased with herself, hitting the Fourex cans at a hundred yards right in the middle of the exxes, and all you can say is *Well*?'

I pick my way through the minefield. 'I was talking about her grammar, not her accuracy.' Why do I feel like Aunt Rube all of a sudden? 'The kid said she was shooting *good* when she should of said *well*.' I pat the head that's bobbing along around about my Plimsoll line. 'Good work, Immo.'

'Thanks,' she tells me. 'Daddy?'

We're near the shack. Dark shadows lie under the rough-hewn pylons and the rickety structure stands atop them like the aftermath of an accident in a nuclear reactor.

'Yeah?'

'When can I learn more about sleuthing than just shooting at beer cans?'

I shrug. 'You're learning all the time, kid. And the name of today's lesson is: *No one's safe nowhere.*'

Mrs Rory doesn't want to be left alone, Roarer's fed up with being holed up on the island, and Imogene's not going anywhere, so I agree to a change of venue – swapping the island for the boat, with Roarer in charge of logistics – while I leave with Monica. According to Roarer, she's got an eye like an eagle, and that kind of talent might come in handy where we're headed.

'I'll drop you back at your joint,' I say to her. There's a nice breeze playing with her skirts while we're standing on the platform, and the usual social security set is slumped in various degrees of depression – dark grey to suicidal. I'm thinking about the past as well as fate and destiny, so figure this is the way to play it, and in the process forget all about consistency. 'I got no right to expose you to danger.'

Monica's eyes rearrange themselves into silver bullets. 'What if I happen to like danger?'

The choo-choo arrives and we climb aboard.

'Everyone wants to be safe.'

'In that case, I'm not everyone.'

Any one of our fellow passengers could be after us – a short-handled knife tucked under their tresses, a sawn-off shottie stuffed down a trackie leg, or a homemade bomb nestled in their underpants.

A way out of the mess would be a one-way ticket to Bullamakanka under assumed identities. But there are two problems with that particular solution – it doesn't take Imogene into account, and there's still the debt I got to settle with Annabel. I glance at the dame as one of City Rail's built-in rock-and-roll curves launches me into her. I straighten myself quick.

'Okay, but you got to do what I tell you to, *when* I tell you.'

'Of course.' The expression on her dial-up's as innocent as a babe's.

So why don't I believe her?

Chapter 19
THE DAME UPSTAIRS

On the surface, Sydney is the destination of choice for the happy set, drawn by all the sun, surf and playful sexuality. On the surface, nicely-behaved traffic works its way neat as toys along clean streets, sailboats scud sweet across an unsullied harbour, and in the wee hours of the morning fun-loving youngsters kick up sandalled feet in a happy and innocent playground of drug-free nightclubs.

If you want surface, subscribe to *The Sydney Morning Horrible*. The *Horrible* doesn't know shit from sewage, gang warfare from a spat in the playground, or road rage from a bout of post-cabbage flatulence. To the *Horrible* there's no underworld and the death of Tommy Tycho's nothing more than an annoying blip in the general Peter-Pan-and-Wendy run of things.

Accordingly, on Day Two after the death, the rag runs this reassuring paragraph on page numero due, the place where the blatt explains what it should have said but didn't, or could have said but forgot to, or tries to sidestep the next libel suit – its ultra-busy Centre of Correction:

And Happy Fantasies, too, to Inspector Leytton. Because if this item confirms anything, it's that the cops are running deader than a flattened maggot in the deaths of both Tommy Tycho and the dame. Another thug's off the streets and they're grateful that someone did the cops' dirty work for them. What if that particular public benefactor might also have taken out an innocent bystander? Call it collateral damage or call it unfortunate. But as Inspector Leytton might put it, *if you know anything that might help police with their inquiries – don't trouble us about it and we won't trouble you.*

We climb off the 412 six blocks early and trawl the rest of the way in our slippers. The jaunt gives me the chance to appreciate yet another of Monica Best's physical attributes. I'm six-foot-plus-something in my socks – the ones with the built-in air-conditioning in them – but the dame beside me doesn't have to look up to me to be on the level.

We've been back to Monica's place and picked up her work gear – a nice skirt, leopardskin tights, and a top that would have been tight on her when she was two – and I'm busy looking the other way when a thought strikes me. Like, where's all the tape – red, blue or otherwise? There's no crime scene, no blue and white ribbon strung all over the place like a cop's Christmas, and no short-arse rozzer hanging around with his hands behind his back singing he still calls Australia home while he waits for the relief shift. There's nothing whatsoever to indicate a murder's been committed.

There's running dead and there's slamming an investigation into reverse. The cops aren't even pretending. Gives me food for thought, while the dame provides the dessert.

'How do I look?'

'Yeah,' I tell her.

'Is that all you can say – *Yeah*?'

On another dame I'd say the words were loaded, but on her they got a laugh attached – a full-hipped, throaty swagger of a laugh that's got me down on my knees on the floorboards and begging for less, a lot less, just at the sound of it.

'Yeah,' I tell her again.

'I can see you're impressed.' She aims for a grimace but misses and comes up with a smile. 'Now if you'd just let me know where we're headed, I can accessorise accordingly.'

The joint's suddenly too small. Someone ought to open the windows.

'We're going to pay a visit to a joker called Petrie,' I say, and she frowns like she's just remembered something. 'Don't worry, you wouldn't know him. He's one of the city's bad men.'

Monica nods thoughtfully as she moves around her apartment, lithe as a cat in her leotards, the sort of creature you can appreciate evolution by, imagine her leaping about the jungle with the grace of a gazelle, the speed of an antelope, and the power of an anthropoid ape – while all she's doing is chucking a bunch of accessories into a side pocket of her anorak.

Before departing, we pay another visit to the floor below. Again, there's no sign of a crime scene. Annabel's door is closed, the fire escape's saying hello to a vacuum, and the seeing-eye in the door labelled 302 – the apartment at the other end of the hall from Annabel's – is unblinking.

I bang on the door anyway.

'Who is it?'

I stand aside from the peephole and motion Mary Poppins to come up with the necessary chit-chat.

'I'm from upstairs.'

The door's opened by a fat man wearing a white stick and shades.

I motion to Mary Poppins again. She nods and asks the question.

'Have the police been to see you?'

'Why would the police come to see me?'

'Because of – what happened.'

'What happened?'

It's clear he's the embodiment of the three chimpanzees – hears nothing, sees nothing, says even less.

'Nothing,' Monica tells him.

'I thought not,' says the blind man, and slams the door.

Chapter 20
INCIDENT IN A TOY SHOP

We're up near Central station and zeroing in on Hephzibah's, when Monica does something that sets my alarms jangling. She sidesteps a thug in a way that suggests she's done the same thing before, a slippy-slide, slow-dipping movement followed by an instant straighten up, like what just happened didn't, before resuming an even keel again – mast straight, sails furled, rock steady, like a beautiful yacht on a smooth sea in the dead-calm aftermath of a high wind.

I hear the echo of my aunt's last words on the subject: *Watch her.*

I shoot her a glance. 'How about providing some kind of back story? Apart, that is, from the bit about the mercenary father that went transvestite after losing the use of his legs.'

She shrugs. 'Private college.'

'After college.'

'Finishing school.'

'After finishing school.'

She looks across and our eyes meet. 'Shift work.'

'Meaning?'

'Security guard, debt collection, bodyguarding, chucking drunks out of clubs, that kind of thing.'

Oh, *that* kind of thing.

'You mean you bounced people?'

She nods. 'Like medicine balls.'

She had a hero soldier for a father and it got in her blood. It would account for all the nice movements. But I still got my doubts. In fact, I got even more doubts than what I started with.

'Look, this is dangerous territory we're entering – even for a hockey front forward, or whatever you were.'

Monica stops and does another shrug. It's a real nice shrug, the finishing-school shoulders rising to form something very much like the apex of an eagle's wings, while the rest of the body stays as still as Venus's did, statuesque in her shell as she rises from the vapours.

'Aren't you forgetting something?' The voice alone would finish anyone. 'Annabel happened to be my friend, too.'

Like a lot of businesses in Sydney, Hephzibah's is no more than a front. The sign above the doorway under the canvas awning says they sell toys. But there are toys, and there are toys.

We enter and the stink of dope – not the opium-derivative variety, but the stuff you put on model aeroplanes to keep them airborne – hits me. It's the sort of stench that goes straight to your sinuses and stays there, then sets about eating you from the inside out, like a herd of starving piranhas. A father's amazing his kid by making a car move without the use of any noticeable devices, because the kid hasn't noticed his dad's standing on a button that activates the electronics. I see they've brought back Meccano.

Apart from the father-son imbroglio and the Meccano, there are a couple of counter hoppers, two mothers and a granny, plus several more kids, as well as scale models of killer jets, military-style tanks that budding Himmlers can trash the lawn with, toy soldiers, a bunch of drones, swords that look like the real thing, too many gats – plus kites to make the joint look as innocent as a cubs' camp – and a shop assistant.

'Yes, sir?'

'I want to see the Dentist.'

'Maybe I can help.'

'And maybe you can't.'

'I mean this *Dentist* you're referring to might be a product we haven't heard of yet.' The kid's fiddling with his iPhone like he means to use it. 'If so, maybe we could try and chase it down. After all, we at Hephzibah's are always on the lookout for new products. Innovation equals expansion and expansion equals greater profits. And in the age of the Global Financial Crisis, greater profits are better than sex.'

If he knows what he's talking about, that makes one of him.

'Are you working at being thick, or were you born that way?' I don't want to hit him, he might break. 'Look, pal, get me Laughing Gas.'

He laughs. 'It looks like you've come to the wrong fun camp, Mister.'

That's when I step forward into him, and that's when the second assistant hauls up alongside. The second assistant's a meat in a black T-shirt that tells me he's kept up his membership in the City gym.

'Why don't you piss off?'

Unlike Monica, the meat hasn't been to finishing school. Accordingly, I don't have to give him the finishing school treatment.

'There's a lady present,' I say quietly. I take his arm and twist it enough to make liquorice out of it. 'Just tell me where I can find the Dentist and I'll let you go.'

The meat reveals a pulse hammering in the vicinity of the occipital. 'He ain't here.'

'And it seems like you want to join him.'

Chapter 21
A TRIP TO THE DENTIST'S

Altercations aren't good for business, so the first assistant starts herding out the mamas and the papas and the rest of the impedimenta. He slams the not-so-innocent door behind them before making the necessary communication on his flapdoodle.

'The Dentist's on his way down,' he tells me.

I let the meat fall to the floor. 'No, he's not.' I haul out the gat. 'On account of we're on our way up.'

Monica's right behind me as I head for the mystery door, the one at the back of the play pen between the Hornby wind-ups and a scale model of a drone, reaching the steps just as the cavalry appears on the landing.

We duck under the stairs and Monica raises one beautiful eyebrow. 'Where are we?'

'This is organised crime *par excellence*,' I say to the tune of the musketry from above. 'This city's carved up like meat and potatoes, and it's not according to culinary taste, either. If Australia's a den of iniquity, then Sydney is Crime Central – some thugs control brothels, others weaponry, while others have got the mortgage on money laundering. Then you've got race fixing, politician bribing and crooked cops – this is the age of the specialist, after all.'

I loose off a slug, and she still doesn't look as surprised as she might be.

'So what's this particular part of the scenery?'

'Dentist's a drug lord. You heard of a guy called Antonio Mokbel? Well, this bastard makes Mokbel look like a choirboy. He controls most of this town's cocaine and amphetamines – ice, speed, juice, whatever you want to call it – and then some. Dentist's to drugs what Sutherland was to singing.'

They're coming for us.

'He's been hauled in several times, but it's only ever been for show. All he does is buy off another copper or judge or politician or offs yet another witness; whatever it takes to stay free.'

Why do I sense that the dame already knows what I'm telling her?

'Go on.'

'Ten years ago he was arrested for importing enough ephedrine to make a billion dollars' worth of ecstasy. Yeah, that's *b* for *bustido*. We're talking some not-so-minor country's entire Gross National Product.'

'Yet he's still at large?'

'He's more than at large, he's bigger than life – other people's.'

That's when the sky caves in. It's like one of those paintings with little men in them – lots of little men, as well as several big ones – down the stairs as well as from the general direction of the toy shop.

We don't go quiet, but we go. My head's playing *The Bells of St Mary's*, while a quick check of the dame reveals she hasn't fared much better, as they haul us up the steps into fairyland.

I judge there's close on an acre of shelving reaching to the ceiling – and it's a high ceiling – shelves packed with boxes and bottles and little white packets with little smiley faces on them, and up and down the aisles run little forklift tractors without anyone driving them, stopping now and again to take down a palette of happy-haps before moving on again, while a non-stop chain-drive rattles around the periphery. Together with the too-sweet smell of an ice-cream parlour. It's Henry Ford's assembly line a century on.

A billion? If this joint's anything to go by, one B would be no more than the tip of a very big iceberg. It's a highway to Hell, and that's where we find ourselves, shoved, prodded and kicked up another set of stairs into a big white room with a nice big, wide window opening onto bleak sunshine.

And in the centre of the room, a black chair.

Monica's on the floor and I'm in a dilemma.

I've been in enough dentist's rooms in my time to know that I'm inhabiting one now, a place full of grey metal cabinets with little grey metal drawers in them and an arc lamp hanging by a giant articulated arm from the centre of the ceiling, while a sweet little nurse in a white mask waits by the chair.

'Would you care to sit?' she murmurs from behind the mask.

'No,' I tell her.

Monica's writhing on the floor, and around her stand a hurtful of hoods clutching too many Uzi machine-guns.

That's when the Dentist makes his appearance, and it's an appearance I don't like. He's got one of those faces you'd expect on a politician or an Emoticon, nice and round with little crinkles around the eyes, the sort that pretends it would never kill you, even if you didn't vote for it. Black hair done ordinary. But it's the threads that give him away. He's wearing a long white coat – the sort they put on shrinks in loony bins – like a kid playing dress-ups, with his sleeves rolled up and neat little feet perched in high-polished pumps poking out the bottom and delicate mitts with a pair of electric-blue Mediflex gloves on them. The kind of gloves favoured by sandwich hands, dentists and murderers. All round Mr Nice Guy.

But I Googie-egged him before we set out and nice guy he's not. Karl 'Laughing Gas' Petrie started life with the benefit of parents, but changed his status to orphan at age eleven, when he killed them. He came from the hard edge of town, the side that specialises in sudden death and general mayhem and too many unwanted pregnancies. His dad was a standover man who destroyed punters dumb enough to object to being stood over, while his mum spent most of her life committing felony and extortion, and being an accessory before, during and after the fact to several murders.

His was a childhood without toys.

It was on his mum's first night out of the slammer after her fourth stint in jail that he killed them – using skills inherited from both sides of the gene pool – shooting them with a sawn-off shottie that his daddy had given him for Christmas. After that, he torched the family home sweet home with a flame-thrower that his mother ditto, to make the affair look like little more than an unfortunate accident. They couldn't pin anything on him. For a start, no one believed he could have done it, he looked so nice.

Hasn't looked back since – graduating to drugs before buying his own toyshop, plus a lot of important people – with the proceeds. Still got his own hair, to all intents and porpoises. Black hair, done ordinary.

He steps into the room and when he does, his army of goons steps aside respectfully.

Monica groans and shuffles her hands in the pockets of her windcheater like she's having a bad dream, after which she rolls back and lies still again.

'So you're Mister Rainbow.' The Dentist adjusts his gloves. 'Pig said you might pay a visit, so I got it all ready for you.'

He looks nice, speaks even nicer. So why have I got this very bad feeling?

'I hope you enjoyed your inspection of our facility.' He smiles, revealing a set of pearlies that any dentist would be proud of. But I've lived long enough not to trust nice enamel work. He plugs the gap in the dialogue. 'I understand you're under the delusion I might have killed someone.' Again the white teeth, simulating what he must think is a smile.

I come to bury Caesar, not to praise him.

'I'm not under the delusion that anyone killed anyone,' I say. 'I happen to know it for a fact, twice over. For a start, you had an excellent motive.'

He gives me his dentist's smile, the one with all the teeth in it. 'Just like everyone else this town.'

'So where were you the day he copped it?'

The Dentist's smile turns into a dentist's laugh. Nice teeth, even right up the back where most people's are rotten. 'I was with Pig, although having the upper hand as I do' – he flaps his plastic-gloved mitts – 'I don't really have to tell you anything. But what I can say is that if I *could* have killed Tycho, believe me, I would have. The bastard took a lot of product from me and never paid for it.' The Dentist holds out his nicely-gloved hands, fingers spread. 'And no one – I repeat *no one* – does that kind of thing to Papa Petrie and gets away with it.'

He nudges Monica with his foot.

'As a result I find myself *personally* not all that unhappy at Tycho's passing. What I am unhappy about is that I didn't *personally* get to organise it.'

'Meaning you didn't do it?'

'You're dead right I didn't do it. And I've got no cause to lie, Rainbow, because after I've finished with you, you won't be in a position to use anything you know against anyone.'

He's moved so close I can smell his madness.

'But we're not here to talk about unhappiness, because they don't call me Laughing Gas for nothing.' With one nice, small hand, he indicates the chair. 'Please be seated, won't you?'

'No,' I tell him. 'You've answered my question, so now I can leave, along with the dame.'

Laughing Gas laughs and this time I figure it's a real laugh so I also figure that this time he's really got something to laugh about.

I bend down to pick up the dame anyway.

That's when I see her eyes flicker and also that she's frowning at me, and not for the first time I figure she knows something I don't – and is prepared to do something about it.

I straighten, step back and find myself in the arms
of the goons that aren't standing over the dame.

Chapter 22
THE TASTE OF PAIN

'Put him in the chair.'

They put me in the chair.

'Hold him down.'

The goons hold me down.

'Now knock out the dame.'

The thugs with the dame look up.

'What'll we use?'

'We've had a run on the Midazolam, so use the narcs.'

A shuffle from the figure on the floor.

'Which ones, boss?'

'Use your head.'

'I thought you told us to use the narcs.'

Something's not computing. Maybe it's a problem with the software, or maybe I just heard wrong.

'Why are you sedating the dame, when you intend operating on me?' I say.

The Dentist does his thing with the teeth. 'All the more reason to sedate her and not you.'

That's when I really struggle but it's to no avail because the goons have got hold of me – one on the legs, two on the arms, and another holding the phyzog – forcing me down into the banana lounge until the only thing I can move is my eyes.

The Dentist turns back to the goons. 'I've changed my mind, let's try the gas.'

The nurse bends over Monica and she's got a black rubber face mask in her little hands and from the mask hangs a long black tube – the sort with bend-wrinkles in it much like the wrinkles around Laughing Gas's eyes – and the black tube's attached to the inside of a black case. And while the goons are holding Monica, the nurse is fitting the mask over her face like she's intent on saving life, only I don't think saving lives is quite what she has in mind. There are a bunch of little black knobs on the case and the nurse starts fiddling with them. I hear the hiss of escaping gas.

'Nitrous oxide.' The Dentist's looking on with interest. 'The anaesthetic of choice in the nineteenth century, and amazingly still applicable now.' He frowns. 'Look, I'm sorry, nurse, I've changed my mind again. Let's use the narcotic.'

The nurse nods, puts away her box of tricks, and reaches for a syringe. At the same time Monica writhes and fiddles some more. After which, the nurse inserts the syringe and she ceases to fiddle.

The Dentist leans over me, his kind eyes glinting. 'Now would you like an anaesthetic?'

'No.'

'That's excellent, because you aren't going to get one.'

That's when the goons tighten their hold and that's also when the Dentist forces something in my mouth, something made of plastic and steel with a ratchet attached to it, something that tastes the way pain always tastes – a mixture of tincture of iodine and mercury and fear – and with each turn of the ratchet, my mouth is forced open wider and –

The nurse shoves a suction hook down against my lower palate while I stare into a big plate-glass searchlight with the word BELMONT in the centre of it, like the bull's-eye in a very big target.

Only the light isn't the target, I am.

'Forceps.'

The dame palms the Dentist a pair of bent-ended pliers and I don't want to know what he's going to employ them for so I try to focus on the light while he's probing. But his face is so close to mine I can't see anything else and I can't smell anything else but the ham and the anchovies followed by burnt toast he had for breakfast, and I can also see the little green flecks in one of his eyes, and it looks very much to me like insanity.

That's when the pain starts.

He's got hold of a tooth in the jaws of his pliers – one of my right upper molars, I think – and he's tugging it like he wants to make a Jacobean chair leg, leaning into the job until the whole world of pain is concentrated in the back of my mouth like it's been inserted through a microscope backwards, and it's waterboarding, electro-voltaic shock, leg-breaking, fingernail-removal, eye-gouging – the works.

The hands of the goon gripping my face could double as snowshoes and he's got a knee in my ribs for extra purchase, when there's a crack, a wrenching snap like the world's been torn asunder, and the Dentist withdraws his fist, and out of the corner of my eye I see the wreckage of what was once my back tooth, a jagged lump of enamel with what might be tomato sauce adhering to it, only I know it's not sauce, it's blood, my blood, and I can taste its bitter-sweet saltiness as it fills my mouth so fast it threatens to choke me.

'Oh dear,' he says, inspecting the tooth. 'There wasn't a thing wrong with it!' He stands back. 'Shock has a curious effect on people, Mister Rainbow, but when you recover, you're going to do me a favour. Find out who killed Tycho, and I'll make sure I give him something for his trouble.'

If there's a logic in all that, it escapes me.

Just like my pearly white.

Chapter 23
IT PAYS TO ACCESSORISE

In my efforts to distract myself from the pain I think of two things:

One: That the steel arm that could hold a rhinoceros might be the key to our escape; and

Two: Roarer said something about *an eye for an eye and a tooth for a tooth*.

I try to work out how the two might go together, except my mind's dulling over, so I focus instead on the word BELMONT in the bull's-eye of the spotlight and tell myself that *Belmont* means *Beautiful mountain*, and I think, *Yeah, mountains are beautiful, they're there to prove yourself on, and also to teach you that what doesn't kill you only makes you stronger.*

That's when the vice closes over my next good tooth and I smell the baby-nappy smell of the Dentist's gloves and see his jaw clench along with the jaws of the extractor like he intends to *bite* the thing out of me without benefit of pliers, and I also note that one of his eyes has turned into a pinprick while the other stays standard, and sweat's beading on his forehead, while the flow of blood to my extremities is ceasing where the goons are gripping onto them . . .

. . . when suddenly the world explodes.

Belmont.

As the cataclysm gathers force, that's what I cling
to, that one eye, a Cyclop's eye, an *eye-for-an-eye* eye
– one pupil a maverick while the other's a piece of
masonry – and I wonder how come I didn't notice it
before, maybe it was because I had other things on
my mind, like what's going to happen to Imogene
when I'm no longer around, not to mention
Monica, who all of a sudden is all over the joint –
a Catherine-wheel, a termagant, a Roman candle,
a factory of fireworks into which someone has just
dropped a match, causing the whole shebang to go
skywards, the goons to slacken their hold on me,
and the Dentist to jab himself with his forceps, as
the dame's right instep collects him across the bridge
of his bugle, the side of her left hand chops down
on goon numero uno's *sterno-mastoid*, her right fist
connects with the *solar plexus* of goon numero due,
while the third goon cops a thump to the ribs that'll
likely require surgery if he's ever going to return to
being upright.

I come out of the space where post-operative
shock puts people and send the Dentist flying into
the oxygen equipment, leaving me to deal with the
fourth goon, giving him a Liverpool kiss plus a
whiteside into the gut.

But I forgot Nursery Girl.

By the time I unforget her she's no longer wearing
a mask but a grimace, the face cover around her
throat and a gun in her mitt and standing nicely
positioned between the chair and the spittoon, while
me and Monica find ourselves between a ratchet and
a hard face, the goons shaking their heads and the
Dentist climbing to his feet with vengeance in his

eyes, where before there had only been madness.

'How did you do that?' He's talking to Monica who's standing in the middle of the floor with barely a hair out of place, looking like she might have come straight from a garden party, the sweetest of expressions on her beautiful visage, legs together, back straight, arms demure by her sides, wrists cocked.

'I went to finishing school.'

'I don't mean how you dealt with the thugs, I mean how you managed to counter the effects of the narcotic, how come you aren't comatose.'

'Moron.'

The goons are back on their feet, the assistant has swung the gun Monica's way, the Dentist's got vengeance at the forefront of his *cerebellum*, and all Monica can do is abuse them.

'Maybe you haven't heard of Naloxone.' She shrugs her shoulders. 'Naloxone hydrochloride is an opioid antagonist, which means it's an effective counter to the anaesthetic effects of narcotics. Naloxone starts to work in roughly a minute, after it's been administered intravenously.'

She's standing like Annie Gets Her Gun and I'm wondering what she's on about, considering Nursie's got the drop on her, while all the dame seems interested in is giving away trade secrets for nothing.

'As it happens, learning from Rainbow that we were paying you a visit – and being well aware of your tendencies – I armed myself with what I might require in the way of protection and when you kept changing your mind I had to keep selecting another antidote. You see . . .'

All eyes are on the hand that's emerging from the pocket of her windjacket, the one with the red-topped needle in it, and consequently no one's paying attention to the hand that's emerging from the other pocket, the one with the gun in it, the gun that she inherited from her mercenary daddy – along with the cold-hearted capacity to kill people.

It's a hip shot and she shoots the dental assistant in the leg and the broad sags down against the banana chair like she's suddenly tired of being a dental assistant, and all that goes with it.

'*That's* an anaesthetic.' Monica's smiling the sort of smile she must have learnt at finishing school. 'Ready to leave now, Rainbow?'

I shake my head. Partly to clear it, but also to indicate the negative. 'I need a minute with our friend here. I want to know who killed Tycho.'

'Brutus Kariakis is the person you're after,' murmurs the Dentist. 'He has access to all kinds of guns, including the type of weaponry that took out Tycho. And he's been gunning for that bastard ever since he relieved him of a cache of weapons intended for the Mafia, and bragged about it.'

'So why didn't you tell me that before?'

The Dentist holds out his hands. He's still wearing the Mediflex. 'You didn't ask me that before.'

'Ready now?'

The dame's got her head cocked and I hear what she's hearing, the sound of clodhoppers on the stairs, and they're not in three-four time, or any sort of time, they're a boiling surf at Bondi and they're on their way to dump us. I figure that's why the Dentist was so forthcoming about Kariakis, he's been stalling after calling up the boys in blue with his electronic gimmickry, the sort of trick fathers move toy cars with, the button on the floor by the chair.

'Wait.' The bastard still wants a favour. 'You gotta tell me – where and when's the funeral?'

It's the same thing Pig asked me, and no doubt for the same reason. But I put the question anyway. 'Why do you want to know?'

'Because I want to spit on Tycho's corpse and dance on his grave. I want to make sure the bastard's dead and see him buried. Is that too much to ask?'

'How do you know we're going to leave you alive?'

'Because I know you, Rainbow. I know that despite the way you dress, you got quality; despite the way you talk, you got style; and despite just about everything else about you, you got a sense of ethics. That's how I know you're not going to kill anyone.' The gendarmes are at the door. 'Now tell me: when and where are they burying Tycho?'

I shrug. 'Keep an eye on the *Wasted and Pasted* section of *The Daily Amoeba*, it's about the only thing the newspapers are good for.' I start for the window, Monica providing cover while whoever's outside is forcing the hatch. 'Or ask one of your friends on Facebook, if you got any, or do a tweet or a blog or a corblimy.'

That's when the world explodes a second time.

Chapter 24
FLIGHT OF THE ANGELS

The thing about being anonymous is you can't allow yourself to get caught. Get caught and they got you – DNA, fingerprints, face scan, blood type, the works. You exist, and the moment you exist, it's game over. It's called identity theft. So when the rozzers bust down the door, I get the hell out of there. The alternative is to file my life in the history books.

I calculate there's a gross of them – that's twenty in the new money but I prefer *gross* – a clutch of state-sponsored racketeers wearing a faded sort of blue-grey nothingness, helmets pulled down over their eyes and wielding everything from hatchets to *Hail Maries* as they spill through the busted-down doorway looking for trouble. Monica's made herself scarce, and it's time I made myself that way, too.

I'm already positioned. The ceiling dangler that's been in the porphyry of my tweedledum ever since I arrived takes centre stage, and all I can hope for is that when the time's ripe, it holds. Madame Blavatsky taught me the flying fandango. Only she had a name for it: *Flight of the Angels*. It all comes back to me – the pad-pad of kids' padded toes in the big room, the stench of dust, and the sweet sounds of Tchaikovsky – as I drop to my haunches, one foot forward, one back, obtaining the requisite equipoise before applying full-thrust, my bodyweight centred on the springs of the gastrocs, quads and *breves digitora* as I launch myself skywards, fingers stretching for the high-point of the dangling arm, as the bastards-in-blue start to swarm.

I feel the robot-arm give as I grab it, a heart-sickening lurch as I give it a load it wasn't meant for – a hundred and eighty-five pound private detective – and the arm jerks down by the width of a broadsword, before the subsidiary anchor attaching it holds, and I complete my trajectory.

I've caught the rozzers off-guard.

Consequently there's a two-second response lag, two precious seconds during which the rozzers' well-drilled minds try to catch up with what their eyes are witnessing, but by then it's too late – too late for them but not for me, as I let go and flip through the window, desperately seeking a safe landing outside.

There's got to be a reason for awnings, and as I plummet earthwards I find it, the shade above the toyshop door just enough to break my fall, before the canvas rips with a sound like a butcher's saw hacking through a steer's skull, and I find myself saying hello to the footpad.

'You all right?'

I'm alive, if that's what Monica means – my arms half-wrenched out of their sockets, a twisted ankle, a battered brain and a tooth missing, but you can't ask for perfect health in this game.

People are yelling.

'You better shelve the equaliser,' I say, trying to catch my breath.

'Sorry, forgot.' The dame pockets the gat and the yelling stops.

'See you at the speakeasy,' I tell her.

It's only after I've travelled several blocks and the cold air's reminding me of the hole where the Dentist mined my grinder, that I remember telling another dame something very similar – *See you in five* – and a spasm shoots through me, because I've just had a premonition: Monica might be about to go the same way as Annabel.

Chapter 25
THE SHADOW IN
THE CORNER

Detecting's a juggling act. A gumboot's got to stay on the move while keeping several objectives in the air without fumbling them. I keep the cerebellum on the target, which is to locate the malefactor. Meanwhile I also got to keep alive, as well as keep Imogene that way. And at the same time, I got to put together all the awkward bits of a thousand-piece jigsaw, while keeping the rest of the act going with grace and fervour.

Dead-man's mobile *numero quinze* gets me Rube.

She's down by the waterfront.

There's waterfront and there's waterfront in Sydney, most of it priced just within reach of a politician that's been extra-kind to the mining industry. Fortnum's is an eatery where you got to produce your bank balance just to get in the hatchway, a joint where the wait-persons wear hard-weave accents, vegetables are listed as an extra – and they make a point of checking the silver before you leave.

'Can I help you, sir?' A thug in black roll-neck, skintights and a tuxedo, with eyes that look like they might have been rolled in a crap-game, is blocking my way. I don't like thugs blocking my way. Thugs blocking my way tell me someone's behind them, someone that's got money that rightly belongs to other people. They also remind me of my childhood.

'Yeah. You can help me by getting out of my way.'

The trouble with social niceties is that not everyone's in the mood to receive them.

'You got a reservation, smart guy?'

When jokers call me *smart guy*, I become what they say I am.

'Have you looked up the word *reservation* lately?' A look of uncertainty smacks into the ugly mug. 'Because if you have, you'd know it's the power of absolution, of keeping your wafer after Mass, and – as a long shot – the land grant by which natives the world over can lie around in the mistaken belief that nothing's altered since their fathers were papooses.' I pause. 'So unless you got a meaning in commoner currency, pal, a reservation's not something I got on me right now.'

I flex the shoulders. Flexing the shoulders reveals the mother-of-pearl composite handle of the Taurus PT940 Special in the crossover holster, the one with the cock-and-lock safety catch, showing what I *do* happen to have on me at the moment, and that it might be worth paying attention to. It's a language the thug understands.

'That would be a table for one, sir?'

'That would be a table for none. I've come to see Rube.'

The look on the thug's face turns to one of respect. 'Who'll I say's here?'

'You'll say no one's here, pal, because that's who I am – no one – and I'm here in person, and in person I can tell her no one's here all by myself.'

Rube's seated by the window, her back to a harbour that's got no hint of what hides beneath – much like the look on her face as I pick my way between all the lawyers, philanthropists, health care professionals, and politicians, as well as all the other thugs that represent the crème-de-la-crime of Sydney society, and therefore can afford to eat here.

'You got to make an entrance, don't you, Rainbow?' she says. 'How many times do I have to tell you that the secret of life is a low profile?'

'He got up my nose, Rube.'

'So what's a nose worth these days? A punch in the face? Your life? Somebody else's?'

I'm a kid again and Rube's my teacher, a dame that knows all the answers before anyone's asked her the question.

'I'm still learning, Rube.'

'We're all still learning, kid – the trick is to stay alive while we're doing it.' Something approaching a smile works its way around her mouth. 'So you found the head man yet?'

I take the query at face value and tell her the state of play. After the food's delivered, it's Rube's turn to provide her take on the action. 'It could still be any of them.' She stares out at the Harbour. 'Every one of those bastards had the motive and they also had the means.' She frowns. 'Even the Widow's not in the clear.'

'But she loved Tycho.'

'Don't wave your fork around, Rainbow.' Rube's

not looking out the window any more; instead she's considering the possibilities. 'She *said* she loved him – there's a difference. Remember that before she became a widow she was a cheated wife. And cheated wives always have a motive.'

'But she said –'

The expression on Rube's face is the same one she had when I did a misstep at ballet, only older. 'What's she going to say, Rainbow – that she did it?'

'But she's got an alibi.'

'Everyone's got an alibi. Only the innocent never have alibis.' She pushes her plate away. 'Now I'll tell you what I've achieved.'

Rube's checked out the bona fides of the bit players, the small fry in the ocean of evil – the whitebait and the yellowtail and the leatherjackets and the rest of the minnows that swim around the mussel-encrusted pylons of mainstream crime, until a shark comes along and they don't.

'And in following up the minor players,' she goes on, 'I'm discovering that every one of them possessed a motive.

'At the time of his death, Tommy Tycho was boffing the Lord Mayor's wife, taking bribes from Dorffmann the developer as well as the union Dorffmann was paying. He owed six-figure sums to Harold Park, the bookie, as well as High Steppin' Annie, the stooge. He was blackmailing a big-league people smuggler as well as a Roman Catholic paederast, and he reneged on a promise to get a Liberal politician preselected and consequently the politician had a contract out on him.' She shakes her head. 'Tycho wasn't what you'd call popular.'

Neither are we, going by a feeling I've just got, but I don't tell Rube that, because Rube would only tell me that feelings don't butter parsnips, it's facts that matter in this world.

'Meantime, I've checked where all these jokers were at the time of Tycho's death and they either weren't in the vicinity or they're a damned sight cleverer than I'm prepared to give them credit for.' She frowns. 'But that doesn't mean peanuts. I'm halfway through the list and it's like trawling through sewers for ice that someone dropped down the S-bend. How long have we got?'

'Two days.'

It's Aunt Rube's turn to look incredulous. 'Two days!'

It's two days before the Widow buries Tycho, two days more that the corpse will sit rotting in her kitchen, after which time – even apart from the fact that it's winter – even the Widow won't be able to stomach the stench.

'Yeah, that's all. By the time of that funeral I need to have all the facts. So, yeah, we got just the two days.'

I avoid looking at the face in the shadows in the far corner of the restaurant. It seems familiar, only I don't know where it's familiar from. It also seems dangerous, only I can't put my finger on why.

'Meanwhile, we got to exit this joint, Rube, like now, and via our respective *lavabos*.'

'Since when were you issuing orders around here, Rainbow?'

'Since I wanted you to stay alive, Rube.' I increase the decibels. 'I'm just going to the john, Aunt.'

Rube answers in an equally loud voice. 'Oh, I do believe I'll follow suit. It seems my bladder isn't what it used to be.'

We get to our respective feet and depart, leaving Rube's bag and my fedora on the *tableau* behind us so that even a not-so-casual observer might imagine we're returning.

Except that after I enter the *Herren*, I depart by way of the *fenêtre*, leaving Rube to make her own arrangements. And the newt in the corner – when they finally realise what has happened – can make theirs.

Chapter 26
A DATE WITH DEATH

Later that afternoon, I meet Monica in a Kings Cross op shop, a joint that's seen better days, a down-at-the-heel hole-in-the-wall crammed with everyone else's mistakes, and smelling like King Tut's chamberpot.

'Why are we here?' she asks.

'Because no one gets murdered in Vinnies.' A little old lady with hair the colour of Paterson's curse is busy trying to flog a fake gold watch to a derelict. 'Vinnies is a lay-by to Heaven, the last refuge of the innocent, the place where guilt comes to die.' I try on a green-and-grey topcoat. 'Roarer's going stir-crazy. So what do you say?'

'It's a bit tight around the shoulders.'

'I'm talking about the boat not the coat. What I'm saying is, how about you taking over dog-watch while Rory joins me for a stint?'

'Do I have a choice?'

I palm the blue lady a shekel. 'Yeah.' Monica's found a skirt that shows more leg than it should, but who's complaining? 'You can either do it, or you can do it.'

She hitches up the skirt to investigate something of interest on her inner thigh. 'Very well then.' She straightens, lowers the dress and smooths the hem, while the blue in her eyes has just got bluer. 'But only because you asked so nicely.'

The *Wooden No*'s where I left her, hidden under an overhanging pittosporum in a jagged-edged bay with others of its Ilkly Moor, her wraparound deck mucked with birdlime and the crack in her hull looking much like the Grand Tuxedo. She's groaning with every movement of the sea as the dinghy I borrowed from among the hundred or so on offer on the shore knocks against her like an afterthought.

'Ahoy there!'

Roarer's head pops out of the engine room, followed by Mrs Roarer and then Imogene.

'Daddy!' Imogene hurls herself over the gunwale. 'You're back!'

I disentangle myself from the kid and my emotions. 'Only for a moment, honey bunch. Just long enough to exchange Monica here for Uncle Rory prior to getting going again.' The kid's gripping something in one of her paws. 'What you got there, sweetheart?'

'My book. It was in that box you put on my bunk.'

'So what's in the book?'

'Important stuff that might help you one day, Daddy.'

Why does it hurt?

'Thanks, darling.'

'Can you stay?' There's mist in her eyes. 'Why not stay and tell me all about your case so I can write it in my book?'

I take the deep breath, but sometimes breaths just aren't deep enough.

'Only when it's safely in the *Solved* folder, sweetheart.' I ruffle her hair. 'Until then, Mum's the word.'

Imogene frowns. 'But Mummy's down in the bilge place, bailing.'

And that's where I find her. Salina's not looking too comfortable in her new environment. Then again Salina never looks comfortable in any environment.

'Aren't you done yet, Rainbow?' She's gripping the bucket, her hair's all over the shop, and her clothes look like they've just fought a losing battle with a mako. 'Hasn't this latest in a long string of emergencies finally drawn to a close, enabling us to return to what might laughingly be referred to as a home, but is Buckingham Palace compared to this – this' – she stares around at the rotten timbers, the broken bulwark and the swill – '*barge*.'

I got to get out of here. 'In just a little while, Salina, I . . .'

'A little while!' She flings the bucket and it misses me by the width of a Gillette. It ricochets off the rusty fuel tank before clattering to a rest by a leaking oil line. 'In – a – little – while!' She hunches into squat that would make a toad green. 'We're supposed to be divorced! I'm supposed to be shot of you! Nobody told me I'd be stuck with you forever! A divorce is a divorce, it's supposed to change everything, give a person a new life! Instead, all I've got is more of the same – only worse!'

It's meltdown time and I can't do meltdowns. I get up to go. 'Look, I'm relieving Roarer,' I tell whoever's in a position to hear me. 'You'll be pleased to know

I'm leaving you another woman. You'll have a lot in common.'

'Are you saying that because we're all women we'll get on like a – like a – a . . .?' She shakes her head. 'You're mad, Rainbow, you been through too much to be anything else. But why the hell do I have to be the one that suffers for it?' Her shoulders sag. 'Oh, just piss off, will you.'

I do what I'm told, and going by the sounds that follow me into the dinghy, Salina's found something else to throw to the four winds, and it's more than just caution.

'Home free!' Roarer's lying back in the bottom of the dinghy in the pale winter sunshine, his brain in neutral where it likes to be. 'You got no *concept* what it was like on that boat, Rain.' He parks his crutch-gun alongside the gunwale. 'It was hell on earth, man, like the Good Lord created the situation as a warning regarding eternal Damnation. They were at each other's throats like the servants of Satan.'

'They're just different personalities, Roarer.'

'They're exactly the same, if you ask me.'

'Sounds like you changed your mind about marriage.'

Roarer shakes his head, but it's a slow shake. 'Only if Salina moves in with us.'

We're hugging the shoreline in order to merge with the environment.

'So what do we do now?'

There'll never be a good time to tell him.

'We're going to see the Brute.'

Roarer's suddenly bolt upright, his one leg shivering out in front of him like an antenna. 'You got to be kidding me. Why?'

'To accuse him of murdering Tommy Tycho.'

Roarer sinks back into the bottom of the boat. 'Yeah, right. Let me get this straight, Rain, or as straight as people can get anything when they're dealing with you.' He's been with Salina too long, his mind's turned. 'You're telling me we're *voluntarily* visiting the town's *mean*-man, after which, and again *voluntarily,* we're going to accuse him of murdering Tycho?'

I don't shrug. It only interrupts the rhythm of the oars. 'He's the last name on the list, Roarer, apart from the minnows, and Rube's taking care of them.'

'The last card in the pack, you mean.' Roarer throws up his arms; he looks like he's responding to a proselytiser. 'That hell boat you just rescued me from suddenly looks like a *sanctuary.* Don't you know that Brutus Kariakis deals ninety per cent of the illegal weaponry in the entire Southern Hemisphere? That he's got more killers at his disposal than the entire Australian Defence Force? And that I'm a flea in his ointment, an annoyance he's wanted to give the flick to for *decades*?'

I shrug. It throws out the oaring but what can I do? 'I got to keep the faith, Roarer. You of all people ought to know that. A dame I owe my life to copped it on my account and I'm duty bound to find the perpetrator.'

'It's a misplaced sense of duty, if you ask me.'

'So do you want to bail?'

Roarer shakes his head. It's a slow shake and a sad shake. 'I guess I'm back in harness, Rain, and therefore I got to go where the reins lead me.' The pun wouldn't be deliberate. Roarer doesn't do puns. He's got his work cut out doing normal. 'And if I die in the doing of it, because I'm doing it for God's sake, it's going to provide me with a one-way ticket to Heaven.'

'You mightn't have to kill anyone, Roarer.'

But Roarer's stopped listening. Instead, he's cleaning his crutch, the one with all the rifling and the bullets in it, pulling down the stock, withdrawing the firing mechanism, sighting down the barrel, and when he talks, it's like he's talking to the gun.

'If it involves Karrybag, it involves killing.' He sights his crutch on a seagull. 'And I got as much faith in that as I got in God.'

Chapter 27
CLOSING IN ON A KILLER

There aren't too many shooting pits left in Sydney, and what there are have got so many regulations you're lucky to have time after the fulfilment of them to loose off a couple of rounds before the bell goes and it's time to pack away the gunnery and go home.

The Brute Shoot's different. It's private enterprise, meaning it's not what you'd call strictly legit, a shooting parlour courtesy of too many shish-kebabs to the local conciliators, housed in a facility that if it was any bigger, would qualify as a city. The only rule is you don't fire at each other – and even that's a rule that's there to be broken.

We approach careful and from the west. There's not much choice in either department, because the joint's built on a promontory jutting out into the Tasman, and the only approach you can make on a late afternoon on a winter's day is slow, and with the sun behind you.

'We could of notified him that we're coming.'

Something's happened to Rory since he found God, not all of it good.

'Think about it, Roarer.' I'm working my way through lantana that's as thick as thieves, with Roarer bringing up the rear. 'What do you reckon would happen if we called up Brute requesting visitation rights? *Oh, Mr Brute, look, me and Rory was wondering if we might trespass on your generosity and pay you a little visit.* You reckon he's going to tell us, *Sure, come on in,* and roll out the Axminster? You think he isn't going to *remember?*'

I wait to give Roarer time to catch up, in more ways than one.

'You talking about the Machine Gun Caper?' What else would I be talking about? 'For Christ's sakes, Rain, that was years ago! And all we did was stop him supplying a couple of hundred Kalashnikovs to a bunch of New Guinea headhunters opposed to a multinational corporation mining virgin rainforest. What's wrong with that?'

I consider what Roarer's just said, plus the hole in the ground that's materialised in front of us, complete with a six-foot-deep razor-trap in it.

'I'll tell you what's wrong with that, Roarer.' I work my way around the trap. 'For a start, it wasn't just a few rifles but ten thousand belt-fed machine guns, complete with a million rounds of ammunition. Not to mention the ten thousand spare barrels that went with it. Second, those ten thousand shooters translated into several million smackeroos. Think how many legislators Brute Force could of bought with that!'

Roarer whacks aside a native azalea. 'Rain, we performed a public service doing what we did. God would of –'

'We're not talking about God, we're talking about the antichrist. And we're also talking about our survival in the here and now, in the only life we can be sure of. We dudded Brute and now you're worried about an invitation. This isn't a garden party, Roarer, we're about to confront the bloke concerning a murder!'

The chain-wire barrier could double as a wombat fence, the mesh descending a fathom into the ground, and the whole affair electrified.

Roarer stares up into the stratosphere, which is about where the wire peters out. 'So how are we supposed to climb *that*?'

Roarer's negativity's one of the changes I've noticed in him since he found Christ, a tendency to look on the down-side of any given situation. Accordingly, I turn my back and haul out the pliers, the ones from the hardware store with the one-shot insulation designed to rot in harmony with the warranty. Always keep the receipt when you buy pliers.

'We're not climbing, we're cutting.' I start hacking. 'Look, I'm paying you good money for this and if you're going to earn your keep, you got to work for it. Pull the wire away after I cut it.'

There's a series of sparks and the shock waves send Roarer stumbling backwards into the lantana.

'You're supposed to be wearing gloves.'

'You might of told me!'

'I just did.'

Roarer's still whining like a tank with differential problems, but after we hack our way through the wire he gets into the swing of things. It's almost like being back with the old Roarer when he belts one of the two mastiffs that come around the corner, while I take care of the other one. They scamper off, tails between their legs.

'That was easy.'

'We're not out of the woods yet.'

Roarer looks around him. 'But there's no –'

'It's just an expression, Roarer. All it means is that we're not there yet.'

'So why didn't you –'

Sometimes communicating with Rory can be like trying to do dialogue with a Martian.

'Look, don't worry about it, okay?'

'I wasn't worried about it until you started seeing trees that weren't there.'

God can't be too fussy if he's taking Rory.

'Just forget I said anything about trees and try to focus on the business in hand.'

We're in view of a building that could house a fleet of jumbos.

'We're making for there.'

'What is it?'

'Keep your voice down.'

We're maintaining cover but we've still got to send a couple of support actors to La La Land and I've no doubt we'll come across a couple more members of Brute's army before we're through.

'It's the gun gallery, the place where Brutus invites punters to test the merchandise before buying, to which he also invites acquaintances for the odd angry shot.'

'I can't hear nothing.'

Rory's heart's in the right place. It's his brain that's gone missing.

'It'd be soundproof, Roarer.'

'I knew that.'

We're on the southern side, the sea a powder-puff

of unreality to starboard, while a seagull's strutting its stuff along the cliff edge. And despite all the masonry and the padded walls and the sound batts I can still hear the soft Victa lawnmower putt-putt of variegated rifle fire, and the not-so-soft thuds as the slugs whang their way into the mounds.

I haul out the Smith & Wesson.

'Provide cover,' I tell Roarer. 'I'm going in.'

Chapter 28
ET TU, BRUTE?

The door opens as I edge my way towards the shooting house. A gat emerges, followed by the thug wielding it. The weaponry finds its way into the polar bear's armpit as he hauls out a Vesta and sets fire to a cigarette.

That's when I hit him. The crack over the skull has got to be the healthier option. After that, I get myself inside – to discover I've just bought myself a one-way ticket to Fantasyland. There's a lot of shouting and the joint's lit up like a turtle on Stilnox. Ahead and slightly to the portside stretches a standful of shooters – a baker's dozen on the rough sum – and they're wearing industrial-size bunny-muffs and goggles, and armed to the bicuspids with everything from Uzis to police-issue Glocks, to World War II .303s, and Vickers' medium machine guns.

Most of the metal they're firing is finding its way into a bunch of objects trundling along the horizon in my peripherals but now and again something lethal ricochets off the bullet-proof glass and goes feral.

I quarter the joint. The cut-outs the punters are shooting at are in the shape of humans – life-sized figures togged out in ties, zoot suits, fedoras, budgie smugglers, frocks, tracksuits, you name it – and while they appear to be walking or running or leaping or just mooching along, what they're really on is an assembly line to eventual annihilation.

Daylight glimmers through holes in the silhouettes like twinkle-twinkles. I tear my peepers away from the ramifications. I'm looking for Brute. Only I don't see him, and Brute's the kind of guy you normally see.

'Why, Mister Rainbow!'

The voice comes from behind, the place where my eyes aren't.

I do a spin-turn. The joker might be built like a smoke stack, but the voice the chimney belongs to hasn't descended to the fire box yet. It doesn't mean I don't pay attention to what the chimney's saying.

'Drop the Smith and Double-Yew for me, would you, there's a good chap.'

Brute — and I know it's Brute, we've crossed scimitars before — talks like a dame out of a music hall, a fluty sing-song of a voice that's got the promise of a great deal of kindness in it, except that the Interdynamic KG9 converted to full automatic he's waving around tells me otherwise. He's looks like a former prime minister — the one that could have walked out of a Damon Runyon fantasy — and is togged out in probably five thousand clams' worth of Ermenegildo pinstripe, no doubt with body armour underneath.

Equalisers are popping off all around me. Bullets are zinging. The floor manager's yelling. You could die of the echoes. I drop the gat.

'There's a good boy. Now let's get back to square one, shall we?'

That's when I see something I hadn't noticed before, and that is that the joint is set out like a play board, the sort of boardgame Aunt Rube would get me to play when I was a kid, to teach me how most people look at life. It's a boardgame with a difference. For a start, it's a dozen times the size of *Moronopoly*. And for a finish, the pretty-coloured properties around the edges haven't got a lot of nice-sounding names like MARYLEBONE STATION, BOW STREET, MAYFAIR and PARK LANE.

Instead they got titles like DEATH and DESTRUCTION, HODDLE STREET MASSACRE, THE END OF THE LINE and THE MORGUE.

'My little joke,' Brute says and prods me past a barred cell marked SOLITARY, while assorted signs read THE GIBBET, ELECTRIC CHAIR and THE SUICIDE OPTION. 'Like it?'

NO GO, NO CHANCE, NO PARKING and DEAD MAN'S CHEST. A rail station marked TERMINAL. Spaces labelled MADHOUSE and DEATHWATCH. The steel-framed door that closes behind us has got a sign on it reading: SQUARE ONE.

'Welcome to sanity.'

Silence, apart from the hiss and fart of a coffee maker followed by a, *Why, hello!* and after that: *How would sir like his coffee?*

The barista's wearing a bulge under his jacket and a fake smile.

'With plenty of caffeine in it.'

Brute shrugs his Ermenegildo shoulders. 'The usual for me, thanks, Bobby.'

He parks his death-dealing machinery on the tablecloth and turns a set of peepers on me that could double as the business-end of a twin-barrelled shottie.

'Look, Rainbow, let's forget little problems like what you cost me in the matter of the machine guns that you quite unreasonably stopped me flogging to the cannibals – plus how you might have got here, and the damage you must have done on the way – and focus instead on the *Why.*' He shoots me what in some circles might pass for a smile. 'I do like focusing, don't you?'

I don't give him the benefit of a reply.

'Oh, dear, it looks like we might need some kind of ice breaker, doesn't it?'

That's when he goes all brisk on me, while I check out the camera at two o'clock high, and the barista.

'Let's start with the layout, shall we? If only to stop you getting any silly ideas. First, the camera you just noticed. It won't hurt to inform you that it's not a camera at all, but a rifle, a 7.62 M134, to be exact, complete with human heat sensor – as provided by an obliging Ministry of Defence – and it's got your temperature on it.'

I shift to starboard. The move's automatic, but so is the gun, its 7.62-gauge snout following me with all the magnanimity of a drone.

Brute smiles a smile that would look better on a corpse, as the barista deposits the coffee. 'This' – Brute waves at the bullet-proof window – 'is the biggest privately-owned firing range in the entire southern hemisphere, New Zealand included. Only Sheik Rhaman Taledi and the Taliban possess better.' I duly admire the scenery. 'That's where my clients try out the merchandise.'

He shoots me a glance – like most fruitcakes he's out to impress.

'I'm only telling you this because I'm afraid that after I tell you, you're going to die.'

He doesn't look as upset as he might be.

'Now an interesting feature of this facility is that each shooting stand possesses an auxiliary firearm that looks very much like that gun you thought was a camera. Would you like to know why?'

I've already guessed why, but I don't tell the fruitcake that. I'd prefer to spend the time I got left working out how to increase the time I got left.

'All right, I'll tell you – it's to give the clients confidence in the product.' He sits back, the skin stretched over his frontal bone glimmering in the arc-lights, nose twitching. 'I've had those little babies programmed to take out the relevant target if a client misses, thereby giving the client the illusion that he hit it. It makes the weapon look good, at the same time making the buyer feel good about himself.' He frowns. 'But I see you're not impressed.'

I shrug. 'I'm not here to be impressed. I'm here regarding the death of Tommy Tycho.'

'Alas, poor Tycho, I knew him well.'

'It's quote, *Alas, poor Yorick, I knew him*, comma, *Horatio*, unquote, if you're trying to do the literary allusion from *Hamlet*.' I resist the urge to make a grab for the gat – judging by the coffee, the joker at the bar's more bullet-man than barista – and instead stay on song. 'Meanwhile, I believe you killed Tycho, or at least were responsible for his death. You had the means plus the requisite motive. But what I'm really interested in, is if you also took out the dame.'

I get a Brutus-type smile for that. 'Rainbow, darling, you know I don't take out dames.'

Well, yeah, the whole world knows that and there's nothing wrong with not taking dames out per se. But I'm not interested in the Brute's sexuality, I just want to know who killed Annabel.

'However, I see what you're trying to say, and the answer is no, no and no.'

I correct him for the second time this session. 'I only asked you two questions, yet you've provided responses to three.'

For that I get a repeat of the smile. 'Yes, I know, but the third *no* is in reply to your unasked third question. And that question is: *Are you going to allow me to live?* The answer to which, as I've already indicated, is – as in the other two cases – *no*.' Brute spreads his mitts, palm up, like he's somebody's saviour, instead of a slaughterman. 'How can I not kill you, Mister Rainbow? First, you trespass on my land. Second, you accuse me of a murder I'd like to have committed, but didn't. And third – most terrible crime of all – you correct my quotations.'

Chapter 29
A VIEW TO A DEATH

He shakes his head. 'In fact, as I see it, the only thing you've done right' – he indicates the view through the bullet-proof glass, the marksmen and the not-so-marksmen firing at the targets outlined against the skyline – 'is that you've come to the right place to be killed.' He smiles the smile of a crackpot from a broken family, whose old man was sent down for killing a cop when he was ten, and whose mother was as crazy as sheet glass whanged by a volley from a machine gun.

'Okay, Brute, given that you're going to have me put down' – one task at a time and the first task is to find out if he did it – 'would you mind answering one last question before you kill me?'

He shrugs. 'Why not? But as I've already told you, Rainbow, I didn't kill Tycho.' He takes a sip of his coffee and grimaces. 'Why do I employ that boy?'

'For the same reason you got the gun cameras – because he shoots straight.' I hunch the shoulders. 'But you haven't answered the question.'

'The question being . . .?'

'Who did it?'

'*Curiosity killed the cat* and you can't catch me out on that one.' The overhead lights illuminate his cheekbones as he leans forward, but they don't get any change out of his eyes. 'All right, while I have to confess I didn't do it – or even cause it to be done – I must say I wish I knew who did, because I'd give him a medal.'

To hear Brutus laugh is to hear vampires' wings whistling in the night, the rattle of shackles in the solitary cell of a condemned man, or the ground opening up under your feet in an earthquake.

'Because, you know what, Rainbow, people like me might be bad, but Tycho was truly evil. Tycho made anything I might have done look like a wrist slap. He aided and abetted my competitors. He took part in collusive tendering. He put the story around that I was flogging second-rate weaponry. He –'

'You haven't answered my question.'

Brute shrugs and shoves away his barely-drunk coffee. It spills on the Interdynamic. It doesn't improve my chances of survival, but it's the answer to my question I'm concerned about.

'That's because I'm afraid that I simply don't know the answer. All I know is that I'd like to attend the bastard's funeral. I want to gloat over his death and urinate on his grave. Above all, I want to make sure he's dead. And talking of dead, Mister Rainbow, it's your turn to take a walk on the boardwalk. Without passing Go. Without even collecting two hundred.'

It's all sky and no horizon as I'm shoved, hands tied, out of Square One, past NO CARKING, and towards the killing zone. At a signal from Brute there's a cease fire. The troop of cut-outs trundle before me – a kid with a spear, an old gent wielding a walking cane, a crone on pogo-sticks, a lawyer with a portmanteau, somebody's mother, somebody's brother, someone else's aunt. Life-sized, two-dimensional human figures set before the wide, blue expanse of the Tasman.

'We've tried our best to simulate reality here.' Brutus is beside me, the ugly little Interdynamic slung over one shoulder, my Smith & Wesson in his other hand. 'The shooters fire into the light instead of having it behind them, the targets are as real as the model people can make them – and of course there's the view.'

I know most of the shooters – in my business I got to – Rastus Nefarius, the Taliban warlord, armed with an Ingram; the Friesan Minister of Defence, General Dolas, fisting a well-oiled Uru Mekanika; Hayley Dools, the bookie, waving a nice little stainless-steel Anaconda; Inspector Moriarty from the Drug Squad, gripping a five-inch Taurus that wouldn't dent a mosquito – but the Narcs have only ever been about appearance; a trio of Triads; a biker; and a couple of contractors.

All here to buy guns, all armed with their weapon of choice, and all keen to try their weapon of choice on this real, live target that's suddenly been presented before them.

I check out Brute. 'Aren't you afraid they'll take a pot shot at you?'

He doesn't pause. 'Now why would they want to do that, Rainbow? I'm the good guy in this scenario, the benevolent uncle, their supplier, while you . . . Anyway, they're the most bloody awful shots. Apart from which, under the fancy clobber I'm dressed head to toe in police-issue body armour.'

We've reached the silhouettes. It's the end of the boardgame. Next square: OBLIVION.

'Now because I'm such a sport, we'll play it like this. I'll leave your legs free and that way you can run any which way you like, and just as fast or slow as you are able.'

'Just like in real life.'

'There's no need to be bitter.' The mortician's features take on a hurt look. 'After all, you were trespassing, and our society doesn't take kindly to trespassers.'

A movement causes him to glance towards the door. 'Hello, what have we got here?'

I know what we've got here without even looking.

They've found Roarer and they're dragging him grumbling and kicking his one leg to join me among the targetry.

I chuck him a look with a fistful of slugs in it. 'You were my last chance, Roarer. What happened?'

They've taken away his crutch-gun, and he's teetering beside me, looking all but naked. 'When I saw Brute I thought you was a goner, so I went down on my knee and prayed to God.'

'Jesus, Roarer!'

Roarer nods like he's seen the connection – only it's the wrong one. 'But they must have seen me on their candid cameras, because they came at me from all directions. What else am I going to do but pray?'

'You could have tried shooting your way out of the situation, like you used to.'

But it's too late to be thinking of yesterday because it's today, and today's full of beautiful scenery, seagulls, and probable death.

The Brute stands back. 'You got a last request, Rainbow?'

I'm standing among the targets propping up Roarer, who's humming *Nearer My God To Thee* because he's seen the Titanic movie a few times too many, and the silhouettes are dancing past at their regulation sixty *pesetas* a minute, and we're about to join them. While no more than a hundred paces distant, the marksmen are licking their lips at the prospect of a duck shoot. The view's behind me. In front I can see the future, and it's not bright.

'Come along, Rainbow.' Brute looks disappointed. 'You must have one last request, everyone does.' He resembles a kid about to open his stocking on an otherwise lacklustre Christmas morning. 'Not even one last message for your little girl, what's her name – *Imagine?*'

He must have been a shrink in a past life, bringing up Imogene.

'No last request and no last message, either.' But mention of Imogene wakes me to the possibilities. 'Okay, I got an offer for you, and it's got two parts to it.'

There's no bullets yet but there's plenty of impatience. Rory hitches his psalm humming up an octave, while I keep talking, on account of there's nothing else to keep.

'Okay, first up you want to know who killed Tycho so you can give the guy a medal. And second up, you want to attend his funeral.' I pause to let those two pieces of intelligence sink in. 'Well, it just so happens I can make both your wishes come true.'

It's a long shot, but long shots can hit the target, you just got to pull the trigger at the right time and hope the wind doesn't drop. Meanwhile, up the other end of the firing line I sense the natives getting restless.

'Why should I believe you, Rainbow?'

I shrug. 'Why should anyone believe anyone? Why should a Yank believe the Stars and Stripes are forever or Roarer here that The Almighty's going to waste Godly time saving him, while the natives are dying in their millions in Eritrea?'

I let that sink in.

'Because people like to believe in stuff, Brute – that's what makes them people.' I do the shrug of a man who likes to believe in stuff. 'It's called blind faith and what else has anyone got in this world? Leave me and Roarer alive and you got hope. Kill us and you got nothing.'

'Are you providing a guarantee with that?'

I nod the nod of a man who'll agree to anything. 'As good a guarantee as you provide anyone you sell a weapon to.'

Chapter 30
COLOUR ME DEAD

'So he lets us go just like that?' Roarer does incredulity better than anyone I know, and he's got a lot to be incredulous about. 'And all you gotta tell him is something he can read in the *Daily Muckraker* anyway?'

I don't look his way. I got my work cut out keeping an eye on the rear-vision. 'Roarer, the shyster was too busy chucking quotations at us to realise what I was up to. Apart from which, there's a price.'

I let that sink in. Give anyone long enough and there'll be at least a glimmer of understanding, even with Rory.

'You mean we got to slip him something?'

He's driving the little green car, the Mazda 121, the one that carries an introductory letter to the mortuary as an inbuilt option, along with the air-bags.

I shake the cerebellum. 'No, we got to go back.'

'Back to where?'

Roarer would have made a nice inquisitor, if only he had a brain to go with all the fervour.

'Back to the Widow's.'

'Why?'

I do the shrug. 'You'll see.' I frown as he makes it around a truck and I realise we just escaped death for the second time today, and by about the same margin. 'But first we got to swing by Rube's, closely followed by a visit to the colour shop.'

The penny – or whatever currency you want to deal in – dropped as I was being frog-marched around the *Moronopoly* board, a certainty that led to even greater certainty the more coloured squares we crossed. Colour me dead, or don't colour me at all.

'Can't you make this thing go any faster?'

'Is God a Christian?'

There's no answer to that so I don't try producing one.

'You got to stop spoiling me like this, Rainbow.' Rube's glance swings to Roarer. 'I thought you'd hung up your crutch.'

In fact, Rory's leaning on it, because Brute handed it back when he let us go – along with the advice that Roarer's crutch is the day-before-yesterday's technology, and if Rory ever wants to upgrade, he knows where to come.

'I might of found God, Rube, but that don't mean I can't follow my vocation. It's in the Bible.'

'Oh, I'm sure everything's in the Bible, Rory. They've covered all bases, haven't they, their little mysteries to perform. But come in anyway.' She chucks the usual look up and down the broadwalk after which we follow her down the hall. 'How's the case coming along, Rainbow?'

'That's why we're here, to see how you're doing.'

She shrugs as she doles out the Kinkara, spilling a little on the table as she does so. 'I chased up all the little fish and they're all waggling their tails in clean water. At the time of the killings, some were in the cooler, some were committing other malefactions, and the rest had alibis you couldn't peel apart with a razor.' She settles the cosy around the teapot. 'It's starting to look like no one killed Tycho.'

After we toss things around without getting any further, and drink Rube's tea, we go back outside.

'Who owns the toy?'

'Roarer got it in exchange for the Caddie, which he donated to the God people.'

Rube nods thoughtfully. 'Someone's not stupid.'

Roarer smacks the steering wheel as we drive away. 'What did she mean by that? *Someone's not stupid.* She was having a crack at me, wasn't she? Saying I'm a dill while the Hillbillies are a pack of con merchants that dudded me. What's wrong with Mazda 121s, anyway?'

I nod at the steering mechanism. 'You just snapped the rudder.' I check the rear-vision, after which I don't check the rear-vision. 'Look, you got yourself a set of wheels, didn't you? With God as a built-in extra. How could anyone call that being dudded?'

I stare ahead, anywhere but behind us.

'Okay, chuck a left here, if this thing can manage it. We need to stop by the paint shop.'

The vehicle that pulls into the kerb two car-lengths behind us is a late-model white Suburu Impreza with heavily-tinted windows. It's the sort of car you can't see into; that people drive when they're killers or cops or just real shy, take your pick. No one gets out of the Impreza and the windows are so black they don't even do reflections.

I bend down to the bubble car. 'Lock the doors, Roarer, and stay in the supercharged getaway car. And keep your crutch cocked.'

I stare straight ahead as I make my way along the boulevard.

Like most product in this world, what the paint shop sells is superficial, something to brighten your daily round with – a cover-up, a lick of balminess to distract punters from the rough side of life, no more than a veneer designed to peel away at the first sign of trouble. Boxes of Spakfilla teeter, drop sheets and rollers and brushes hang out along the walls, along with a bunch of grey gasmasks that look like leftovers from yesterday's nightmare, and the guy coming from the counter doesn't look like the brightest patch on the colour chart.

'Do you want my advice, sir?'

He's long and he's rangy and he's got a bald spot, and also what looks like purple paint on the bald spot.

I rearrange the Smith & Wesson. 'Why do you say that?'

'Well, you know, the clothes . . .'

'I'm after a colour chart.'

'Why do you want a colour chart?'

There's a car outside wearing wraps, not to mention a couple of murders waiting to be solved, and a heap of crooks is waiting for me to break a promise, while a bunch of broads is sitting vulnerable on a boat – and this turkey's making like he's Eddie McGuire in *Who Wants To Be A Dimwit*. But you learn self-control in this game. Lose that and you say goodbye to your right to keep on living. Accordingly, I don't lift the turkey up by the wattle and shake him. Instead I tell him an answer.

'It's to add a dash of colour to my otherwise lacklustre life, and also to lift my gun sights over and above the mundane level of hurting people.' I shoot him the hard look. 'What's it matter what I want it for?'

'I'm sorry, sir. What colour do you have in mind?'

'Orange.'

'Orange?'

'That's what I said – orange.'

'I'm afraid there's no such colour as orange, per se.' He ups the half-smile to three-quarters. 'So if you can't give me more of a clue than just *orange*, I'm not sure I can help.'

I'm running out of patience, not to mention time. 'Palm me a colour chart, pal.'

So he palms me a chart and when I open it, I see what he's telling me – there's no such colour as 'orange'. They got Cinder Glow and Citrus Combo and Outback Gold. They even got Orangeade. But they ain't got orange.

'You ain't got orange?'

Mr Paint shakes his brain. 'I'm sorry, sir. Like I said, we have Calendula, Sabre Sun, Coppersmith and Golden Koi, but there's no such colour as orange.'

I hear it coming in my head – a nursery rhyme – and I talk to frighten it away. 'What do you mean, *no such colour as orange?*'

'Multinational market research advises us that names like *orange* simply defy successful marketing. People don't buy ordinary any more. Ordinary died with the horse and buggy, lead paint and good manners. There's just no such colours as *red* or *yellow* or *blue* or – Heaven forbid – *orange*. We're not selling paint, sir, we're selling dreams – and the dreams people buy are the names.'

I got the nursery rhyme stuck in my brainpan and I also got what this joker's telling me, and together they don't make a pretty picture – whatever name you want to give it.

'It's not us,' he goes on, 'it's people. The paint company even gives us lectures on the subject. *You're not selling colours*, they tell us, *you're selling names – names like Golden Shower and Subtle Moonbeams and Shifting Sands and Sang Froid*. So I'm sorry, but basic orange has gone the way of the boomerang and the nulla-nulla. If you want green you're out of luck. But we could do you *Robin Hood* or *Sheer Envy*. Now is there anything else?'

'Yeah, palm me one of them respirator things.'

The Impreza's still in place. I note the licence plate and text it to Rube via one of the dead-men's mobiles. Then I tell Roarer to get out of there, fast.

'This thing can't do fast.' He chucks a look at the respirator. 'What's that?'

'They probably call it *Several Shades of Grey*.' The Subaru's tight in behind us. 'Come on Roarer, step on it.'

'I am stepping on it, but it's like treading on a snail.'

Sometimes Roarer gets it right. I drag out the equaliser and haul down the *fenêtre*.

'So what's it for?'

'What gats are usually for.'

'Not the gun, the grey thing.'

We haven't got a chance in hell of losing the tail any other way so I shoot out the left front Dunlopillo and the Impreza swerves to port, mounts the kerb, and ceases following us. I pull my head in.

'It's for my own personal use and gratification, Roarer. Now shut up and chuck another left, then a right, then left again.' A check in the rear-vision shows that – for the moment anyway – we're in the clear. 'And if you can't go any faster, we can always drop into Hephzibah's and borrow a wind-up key.'

Chapter 31
IT ALL COMES TO A HEAD

The Widow's lost her taste for colour and is wearing black – black hat with a veil held up off it, black dress that covers everything but her hands, black stockings, black pump-ups, black look.

'Oh, I didn't expect to see you again, Inspector.' Her mood matches her garb. 'And this would be . . .?' She's looking at Rory.

'He's Short.' I figure I better elaborate. 'That's Detective Senior Constable Short.'

The Widow drops the veil, and if she's got an expression on her dial-up, I can no longer see it. 'I knew the police had changed the height restrictions but I didn't think they'd ever descend to . . . I'm sorry, it's the police force's business, not mine. Come in. And if you notice a smell, it's just some toilet fragrance I sprayed the place with, because my neighbour complained.'

It's hard to know what's worse – the pong that was here before, or the stuff she's overlaid it with. I drag Roarer in by the shoulder pad.

'What *is* it?' he whispers.

'It's Tycho,' I tell him. 'She's got him parked in the kitchen prior to burial.'

'But he's gone bad!'

'He was born bad, Roarer. Besides, it's winter, and corpses decompose slower in cooler weather.'

'I'm sorry, what was that?' The Widow's got mourning rags over all the furniture and black crap covering the window, and as a result the joint possesses all the cheery ambience of a graveyard.

'Constable Short was inquiring as to the date of your late husband's interment.'

She hunches her shoulders under all the crappery. 'Oh, dear, I'm afraid that's become something of a problem.' She leans forward on the couch. 'I've had a lot of people here, including the lovely folk from Bright Lady, and Cheapa Funerals, and they all say the same thing – Tommy's too hot to handle.'

'They were being metaphysical.'

The Widow stiffens like she's been starched. 'I don't see how that could be, Inspector, because that would imply Tommy was somehow . . .' She doesn't say how Tommy was somehow. 'No, I believe they were referring to the smell. I don't notice it, of course, because he's my darling Tommy and that's all that matters, head or no head.' She pauses. 'No, that's not all that matters. I want a Christian burial. Tommy deserves it.' She looks like she's frowning under the veil. 'Only I'm finding that true Christians are thin on the ground when it comes to headless burials.'

She's playing Roarer's tune.

He leans forward, hits the smell barrier, and rears back. 'You say you want to bury him?' His voice is nasal on account of he's clutching his nose. 'But no one will take him?'

'That's exactly what I'm saying. The last people suggested I call up a garbage truck, with one of those dumpster things they park in the gutter, and get a cherry picker and just dump him in the dumpster and cover him with builder's refuse and have him carted away to the tip.' The Widow's looking upset, even under the veil. 'Well, I couldn't do that, even if it were legal, which I very much doubt it is. But as I said before, people are starting to complain.' Her hands play tiddlies in her lap. 'Oh, what can I do?'

Rory adopts his beatific look, the one that says that with the help of God and a bit of money and the Hillbillies he's capable of just about anything. 'I reckon I know how and where you can bury your husband, Mrs Tycho.'

I hear the sound of a motor arriving, and I figure the time that's elapsed since we last saw the car matches the time needed to change a shot-out tyre and get to the Widow's afterwards. I also figure I can follow Roarer's thought processes, which is about as difficult as tracking a black rat over a white corpse in broad daylight.

'I happen to belong to this church, see, and I know they'd be only too happy to conduct the funeral for you, for a little consideration. Do you happen to possess any funds?'

I can't see the Widow's face but by the set of the shoulders and the sudden straightening of the pigeon back I suspect she's offended.

'Nothing but the widow's mite.'

Roarer nods. 'They'll take that. It's in the Bible. *And there came a poor widow and she threw in two mites.* God's happy to take anything you got, if that's all He can lay His hands on. My church will bury your husband for you.'

'Oh, would they?' The Widow claps her hands.

'Would they really, Constable Tiny?'

Roarer ignores the implication. 'I been to some of their funerals and they put on a real good show. I'll arrange it all for you.'

The Widow claps her hands again. 'Oh, would you? And after he's buried, would I be able to join this beautiful church of yours?'

Roarer must be on some sort of commission.

'Yeah, I can arrange that, too.'

I stand up. Like they say, matters are coming to a head. Suddenly I got to get out of there, and it's not just the smell. But first I got a couple of questions.

'When are you going to refurbish? You remember I found a piece of paper with a word on it, and you said it was the colour you were painting the joint.'

The dame's on her feet, too. 'That's right, I did, didn't I?' She's got us to the hatchway and it's like she's trying to push us out. 'In fact, I'll be painting the house right after Tommy's taken care of, it will help in the marketing.' If she believes that, she'll believe anything. 'That's the reason for the piece of paper you found. I was working through possible colours.'

'And the colour – refresh my memory – is *lemon?*'

'Oh, certainly not, Inspector, it's *orange.*' The Widow seems to have a burst of inspiration behind the mosquito netting. 'After all, it was our favourite colour.'

'I guess you checked with the paint shop around the corner that that's its name – *orange?*'

'Oh, yes . . .'

I got that settled. But there's one more thing before we go. 'I need to pay my last respects to Tommy.'

Roarer opts to stay where he is, while I slap on the mask, replace the hat, and go in.

The body's still there and it still doesn't possess a head and despite the cool weather and all the sprays – insect and toilet and maybe embalming – and even with me wearing the mask, the remains of Tommy Tycho still stink to high heaven. I do the visual. And on the greying flesh below the Plimsoll line, just beneath where the head was blown off, I can still make out the words *Populus vult decipi*, and I can also still remember how the phrase translates from the Latin: 'The people wish to be deceived, so deceive them'.

I complete the circuit, commit the rest to memory – which is the one word, *decapitare* – before getting the hell out of Hell's Kitchen.

I tip the fedora. 'See you at the funeral.'

'What did you say?'

I take off the hat and the mask. 'I said, *We're going.*'

As I replace the fedora on departure, sheer instinct makes me drop on the turn, and the slug that takes out the hat and whangs into the architecture's a big one.

The kind of slug that, like Pig said, if it was in your garden you'd call in the cavalry.

Chapter 32
A GOOD DEAL OF DEATH

I haul out the equaliser and fire off a couple of shots as the Impreza accelerates away, its darkened windows sliding to the *rack-off* position and its tyres spitting fire. They're quick bunnies, Imprezas, unlike the Tonka Toy, and by the time I get a bead on the wheels, it's too late.

'Who was that?' Roarer's emerged on the stoop beside me, clutching his honker.

'I believe it's the joker that took out Lover Boy.'

'Lover Who?'

I could stick a fist in the aperture the slug made.

Same with Roarer's cakehole.

'Same kind of gat.' I'm talking to myself more than to Roarer. 'Same kind of slug.'

The Widow looks up the carriageway after the Impreza. 'Oh dear, do you think they'll be back?'

I shake the head and nod it all at the same time. 'Is the Pope a Protestant?'

The case is gathering momentum. I climb into the car. It's time to arrange someone's funeral.

'Next stop, the Killjoys.'

Roarer clashes the gears. 'It's the Hillbillies, for Christ's sake, Rain, the name of the church is the Hillbillies, and I don't find anything funny about getting the name wrong and poking fun at them all the time. They gave it that title so they'd attract the ordinary punter.'

A phone playing the theme song from *Spartacus* saves me from answering.

'The Subaru's hot.' It's Rube. 'Stolen from outside an early-morning eatery in Bridge Street where the cop that owns it was purchasing coffee and croissants, and it hasn't been seen since.'

If the road to Hell is paved with good intentions, the journey to the Church of the Latterday Hillbillies is a billycart ride. It's a great barn of a place set among rolling hills on the highest hill around – a bunch of tombstones, a garden landscaped to within an inch of its terrestrial life, and trees scissored into the shape of angels – all stained-glass *fenêtres* and crosses and flying mattresses and a roof as steep as current-day electricity charges.

The minister's tilling the graveyard. Rory crutches across the paddock to him, and I follow.

Rory goes all shy. 'Hi.'

They embrace. I wince. Roarer's supposed to be a killer, yet here he is doing the full-body thing with a minister. Roarer steps back from his embrasure.

'This is –'

'Smith.' I don't give him a chance to call me whatever it was he was going to call me. 'Mr Smith.'

The minister smiles the smile of the broad church, and I take a step back before he tries to do to me what he just did to Rory.

'Smith, did you say?' He looks from me to Roarer and back again as he drops his trident and raises his arms from the empty-hug position to the sort of gesture St Francis might have used when he was blessing unsuspecting animals. 'So you'd be brothers?'

It's my turn. 'In my world, Preacher, everyone's brothers.' I straighten the shoulders. Putting the gat on display isn't appropriate to the occasion. 'We're here about a funeral.'

'Yours or somebody else's?'

I don't laugh. Laughing only encourages them.

The preacher coughs. 'Yes, of course, certainly we do funerals.' He fingers the 38-carat gold cross on the 38-carat gold chain around his one-carrot neck while I hunch my body around the .38 in the shoulder holster. 'Would the deceased have been a believer?'

'Is that important?'

'It makes a difference to the emolument.'

'The moll I *what*?'

'The cost of the funeral.'

I'm back on song. 'What kind of a difference?'

'Non-believers cost more.'

So I tell him, 'Yeah, the body was a believer.'

The minister's a pork pie of a man, long grey hair done in a horse's tail, fat figure all wrapped up in shorts, singlets and sincerity, but I got to believe he's a preacher on account of the cross.

'Right. Would you like the standard ceremony or the deluxe?'

'What's the difference?'

'About ten grand.'

I chuck Roarer a glance but the monopod doesn't look as perturbed as he might be.

'Am I still in the black?' he says.

The preacher looks down at his fork. 'I believe you're as black as anyone can get.' He coughs again. 'After all, you gave us your house and your car and all the money you had in the bank.' He inclines his head. 'So, yes, almost certainly, and without even looking at the books, I'd say you could afford the standard.'

I feel more nauseated than I did in the presence of the corpse.

Meanwhile, Roarer's still busy negotiating. 'How many Heavenly Credits do I get?'

'Let's see.' The shyster pretends to think. 'I'd say about seven.'

'And how many do I need to get to Heaven?'

'Ten should see you through.'

'Do we book him into a graveyard?'

The Preacher waves behind him. 'For a little extra we can bury him here.'

I shake my head as we make our way back to the Cyclops toy. 'Are these jokers on the level, Roarer? He's taken your house, the Caddie and all the money you got in the bank. Hand the bastard a shooter and he's a crime tsar.'

When Roarer shakes his head I can hear his brain rattle. 'You got it wrong, Rain. You haven't heard the bastard sing. Dames have been known to swoon. The most Highly Reverend Pentecost is truly blessed.'

'Yeah – a blessed shyster.'

In the rear-vision I notice him looking after us as we leave, like he's afraid we might deface one of his death stones on the way, or tear up one of the angels.

But that's not what I'm looking at.

Behind the preacher I can see the snout of a vehicle that's more than familiar, the bonnet of Rory's pink Caddie, parked halfway between the church and the mansion behind it.

But that's not what I'm interested in, either.

I'm more interested in is what's humming in the greenery.

And it's not bees.

It's the Impreza.

Chapter 33
THE HOLE IN THE HARBOUR

I'm a juggling man. But unlike the jokers you see with their fedoras upturned, an emaciated canine or a kid beside them and a forced smile on their dial-up, I'm not throwing rubber bouncies in the air, I'm juggling lives. A whole lot of jokers have got a whole lot of reasons for following us. To the crime bosses I've been paying visits to, you can add the myriad of smaller fry that Rube's been checking up on. After that, you can factor in the cops, the crims I've crossed over the years, people I owe money to, and jokers that just don't like my face – not to mention the bastard that took out Tycho and Annabel.

Added to that, there's always Pandora.

And . . .

Winter's why the body in the Widow's kitchen hasn't turned completely putrid, but it's not the reason my blood suddenly goes colder than a corpse in a mortuary.

'Step on it,' I tell Roarer.

'I am stepping on it.'

'Then step on it some more.'

'Look, Rain, these babies might go slow, but the upside is they're dirt cheap on fuel.'

'And seeing that the Right Reverend Dolittle's ripped you off so bad, you got to save on fuel, right?'

'Why've you got to go on about it all the time?'

Darkness is looming and the tide's receding when we get to the pontoon. I'm starting to wonder if my tide – as well as that of everyone else near and dear to me – is about to go on the ebb as well.

We've managed to lose the Subaru but I haven't lost the feeling we're in more trouble than a drunken nun at a christening.

We commandeer a dinghy that's still got its bung in and start rowing and I phone Rube on one of the untraceable mobiles. 'I want you to check out the dame.'

'Got a name?'

It's then I realise I got nothing on the dame but suspicions. 'I got a name but I suspect it isn't the right one.'

'So give us a lead.'

'We got an address, the joint above you-know-who's place, and an address always comes complete with a name – like an owner or a renter or someone with a mortgage. From that point, we can get a handle on the dame. The address, in code, is as follows.'

Talking of addresses, I gave the preacher the address of the Widow so they can attend to the details – decide on the songs and the sentiments to be expressed and the rest of it – and we've swung by the Widow's and told her to expect a visitation and now we're on the way to the *Wooden No*, where I got no idea in the wide blue yonder what awaits us.

I realise I don't know Monica Best from a box of socks.

She turns up in the apartment above that of the dead dame.

Fortuitous.

She's got a gun.

More fortuitous.

And apart from all the lucky strikes above, she turns out to be more than handy with said gun, as athletic as any Olympian, and a more than willing participant in the various nefarious activities I employ her in. And I've left her in charge of the kid.

Like Rube said, it's the eyes. Show me a beautiful dame and my brains go out the window. Give her a pair of peepers to go with the beauty and I'd murder my mother for her. All right, so that's not going to happen, because I've never possessed a mother, but –

We round the first cove.

Roarer's rowing and I'm perched on the pointy end of the coracle with my gat out, scanning the horizon like Ozymandias – and I wish I didn't think that, because as soon as I think that, the words of the poem pirouette in my skull like a murderous fairy:

'My name is Ozymandias, king of kings: Look on my works, ye Mighty, and despair. Nothing beside remains. Round the decay of that colossal wreck . . .'

'Faster, Roarer, faster!'

'Rainbow, I'm rowing as fast as I can!'

I could call Salina, but that would only alert Jezebel that we're coming.

Theory 1: She killed Tycho.

Cancel that theory, as she was in her apartment at the time.

Theory 2: She killed Annabel.

Put that particular theory on hold.

Meanwhile she's got Imogene.

It's a long row, longer on account of my suspicions, tacking in and out among the bird-limed hulks that clutter the byways and why-bays of Sydney Harbour, and all the rats and fleas and barnacles and other creeping low life accompanying them, reflecting the ups and downs of their owners' misfortunes – 60-foot Halvorsens, twin-engine Gypsies, broken-masted windjammers and tattered-hulled tubs, cats with one keel in the grave and the other in Davy Jones's locker, and ocean goers that look like they couldn't even handle the Harbour on a nice day.

And buried among them, the *Wooden No.*

I've spent half my life hiding that tub from danger, only to invite danger on board, along with the kid. I shove Roarer aside and take over the rowing. It doesn't make us go any faster but at least it gives me something to do, the in-and-out rhythm of the oars hauling me ever deeper into Hopeland, and I'd give Roarer's God everything I haven't got and then some, in return for whatever He can do to save Imogene.

We've got around the fifth promontory, heading north-by-east.

'It's all right, Immo, we're coming.'

'What did you say?'

I shrug myself back into the oars. 'Nothing.'

'You said something.' I can't see Rory because he's in the bow and I'm rowing, but I can feel his eyes casing my back so I clam up. 'You're not praying by any chance are you, Rainbow?'

I tell him to shut up and after that I paddle faster.

The voyage still takes forty-seven minutes twenty by my chronometer, but a century might have passed by the time we round Cape Hopeless – where at low tide you can still see the tip of the masts of the schooner it's named after – and find ourselves face to face with where the *Wooden No* was.

Was.

I stare around.

Nothing.

A few white-topped wavelets, the ragged reflection of a lighthouse, the bent shadow of a straggly-gum, a spectrum-smear of oil on the surface of the water.

But apart from that, nothing.

Then I spot it, rocking gently, and my brainpan lurches along with it, amid all the muck and grime of not-so-distant memory, a little girl gathering her treasures about her the way an old dame clutches her skirts when the wind lifts – toys, a rusty bobbin, the book she's writing . . .

Like a drowning man, I'm lying on my stomach in the crap room at Saturnalia's, and the kid's fussing over her box of goodies like she's busy collecting knick-knacks for a jumble stall. Puts me in mind of Pandora's box of tricks, Imogene's tin of goodies – an old Arnott's biscuit tin with a silly looking parrot on the lid, balanced unsteadily on one claw while the other's clutching a Milk Arrowroot.

'No point hiding stuff where no one can see it, sweetheart. You want to keep everything above board in this world, and your hands on top of the table.'

Imogene hunches her narrow shoulders inside the

fairy-floss skirt, and when she shakes her head, the purple-and-yellow clasp holding the ponytail rattles like a machine gun. 'But Daddy, if I've learnt one thing from you, that's just what I *shouldn't* do.'

'Shouldn't what?'

'Tell everyone everything.'

'So what should you do?'

She deepens the voice, and does a fair imitation of a certain private detective. 'Don't tell nobody nothin'.'

She's good, I'll give the kid that, like I'd give her a lot of things if I had them. No one's pushing her around, not even her paterfamilias.

'I still don't recall teaching you anything about tin boxes with parrots on them, kid.'

A nod of the head, machine-gun rattle of the hair gripper. 'But you *did*. You always said that nothing's permanent. *Nothing's forever, kid*, you told me.' Again the voice. *'And you better believe it.* So I've been putting everything in my box – my best doll, the rat skeleton, the book I'm writing . . .'

'Oh, yeah, the book.'

'That's right, Daddy, there are some things I want to keep forever . . .'

Chapter 34
LADY GO NAKED

The water's icy, chilling my blood along with the thought that this might be all that's left of the kid – a parrot-topped box bobbing among the waves, with water dribbling off the beak of the bird like angel's tears.

I get back to the boat and with trembling hands prise open the lid which has been sealed with plasticine, fishing through the contents, like I'm scrabbling through betting discards well after the last race has been run.

And this is what I find:

A fairy picture.

A ferret's skull.

Assorted miscellanea.

The book.

The ink smears as I flicker through the pages, until I come across what I'm looking for:

'I'm writting this in my cabin where the
man in the mask locked me, using the light
of my lady detective's torch to write by.
He came for us at midnight but I couldn't
see his face because of the mask. The lady
tried to save us with her gun but the mask
man grabbed me and held me in front of him
and told her to drop it or else, so she did.
Then he put mummy and Janet and the lady with

the gun in the aft cabin and me in my cabin in the
proud where I'm writing this and when I heard
him start the motor and felt the boat move I knew
what I had to do so I'm putting this in the tin
box and after that I'll put Blue-Tack around the
edges so water can't get inside and throw it out
the porthole and hope that sum-one finds it.
I figger we're heading east . . .'

*Man in a mask . . . lady tried to save us . . . heading
east . . .*

It's like a message from the grave. Only there ain't
going to be any graves, not where Immo's concerned,
not if I've got anything to do with it.

'We got to borrow a boat.'

'We already borrowed a boat.'

'Not a tinnie, Roarer, a big one, one with a donk
in it, a stink boat, a launch. We're going to need
power, and a lot of it.'

It takes a while but we eventually find one – a
metal launch called *It's a Steel* tucked away next to its
tombstone buoy in this watery graveyard, an Island
Gypsy with just enough in the battery to start the
135, an engine capable of producing eight knots on
a good night, although this night's shaping to be
anything but good.

We come across the *Wooden No* up by the quarantine
station, out near the open seas, and one step short
of the Harbour floor – almost on the rocks, because
whoever brought her here cut the cable and left her

to scuttle herself before they departed.

It's started to rain and the seas are up and Janet's down on her housemaids on the outer deck praying to God Almighty, Sal's screaming, someone – it must be the kid – is trying to start the engine, while Monica has discarded what remained of her modesty and is poised on the prow to leap into the briny, wearing a greasy hempen line around her waist, and little else worthy of mention.

Past the mist of rain, Imogene appears in the stern, wet hair plastered over her face, and waving. A yellow-and-black buoy is near enough to be useful and I can see that's what Monica's aiming for. But I'm looking anywhere but at Monica, yelling to Roarer to shove the *Steel* into reverse before tossing a jury-rigged anchor over the portside to Imogene.

'Grab it, Immo!'

The storm's increased and so has the urgency.

The tiny figure scrabbles for the lifeline.

'I've got it, Daddy! But it's too heavy!'

Roarer's got the *Steel* treading water, but the *Wooden No* looks like the water's about to tread her. She's heading for the rocks. Monica's stroking out among the choppy waves, but she can't make it to the buoy, breaching like a mermaid before turning back as I hear the jury-anchor rattling out of Imogene's hands along the deck on its way to uselessness as the *Wooden No* lurches towards the shore, rocks clawing out towards the old tub with Imogene on it.

Imogene and –

'You okay, Salina?'

'Piss off, Rainbow!'

That accounts for Salina, while Janet's still praying and I can see the cable coiling around Imogene's legs ready to take her over the side of the *Wooden No* along with the anchor.

Monica's drawing abreast of me as I launch myself over the great divide – *phalanges* reaching into air to curl around the *Wooden No*'s railing – as the hull crunches into the rocks.

It's the end of the line. Up Whatever-creek without an outboard, fists gripping the railing of the *Wooden No* as she lurches further rockwards, legs flailing helplessly in the water behind me.

Sorry, Immo.

Who had much more faith in her father than he was worth.

But that's when I feel a pair of vice-like hands clasp my uncles and I know whose hands they are. I force myself not to visualise what's attached to them as Roarer increases the tempo of the *Steel*'s engine while chucking it into reverse, and every atom of my anatomy from my *trapezia* to my superficial transverse ligaments screams with the strain.

I can feel my knuckles crack as they attempt to drag themselves loose from their sockets, along with the *humera*, the *radia*, and the *ulnae*. The two vessels are joined and once one of them's on the rocks we're all gone, lost forever in the torment of the seas and the hungry jaws of the sharks, with nothing remaining but the odd head, a foot, an arm, and a box of biscuits with a parrot on the lid.

I force my mind into reverse, along with the purloined boat's engine. We're not done yet. I'm strong enough to hold the *Wooden No* and it looks like Monica's strong enough to hang onto me. But will can only go so far. After that, it rapidly becomes *won't*.

I feel my fingers slipping and Monica's grip loosening, while the sea around us has turned into a battering ram, and the boats I'm slung between the wheels of a rack.

'I've got it, Daddy!'

As the boats lurch on the cusp of certain disaster, I see the small figure snarl the anchor around the stern capstan, a determined little figure with what looks like blood all over its determined little features.

I yell at Roarer. 'Okay, go for it! Give it all you got! More power! An Island Gypsy ain't a 121!'

That's when Roarer puts the stolen craft into overdrive – an ear-splitting roar that drowns even the wind – and the lurch as the strain takes charge of the boats tears my uncles out of Monica's grasp and I see the stern of the *Wooden No* spin around towards the rocks before rearing upwards like Janet's God has decided to ditch the Ethiopians, arresting the tub within death's breath of its date with Destiny.

The *Wooden No*'s bow takes a dive as the twanging cable that Imogene managed to snarl in the capstan twangs taut under me, flinging me skyward, and the last thing I see before I smack back down into the shark-infested seas is a small, pale face leaning over the side of the tub, staring fearfully down at me from a busted railing.

Chapter 35
DEAD MEN DO TELL TALES

'So who did it?'

The wind's subsided and with it the seas, and we're back in the comforting embrace of the upside of the Harbour. We've untangled the jury-anchor from the *Wooden No* and found safe anchorage after re-parking *It's a Steel* back where the owner can find her.

Salina's settled as much as she's ever going to settle and Janet's stopped praying and Rory's doing a one-legged strut like he's just saved the world. Imogene's checking the contents of her parrot box to make sure none of her past's gone missing, and Monica's wrung the last of the Harbour out of her clobber and got respectable.

Sparks fly in the early dawn light as she runs her fingers through her hair. 'I think it was some rich kid with too much time on his hands.' She has another go. 'I mean he didn't kill us outright.'

'You still would have been dead.'

She frowns. I can see she blames herself. 'He had Imogene. Anything could have happened. I did what he told me to do.'

'Did you get your gat back?'

She nods her electric hair. 'He didn't care about the gun. As I said, he struck me as a Hooray Henry who wouldn't know his *glutea maxima* from his *humora* – with a mask on. Look, I know you came looking for us because you were suspicious of me and quite frankly I don't blame you.' A breeze is whispering among the black trees on the shore. 'You find me in a place I shouldn't be in, carrying a gun I shouldn't be carrying, and capable of acts I shouldn't be capable of.' Her peepers on me are like the caress of the breeze. 'You have a right to your suspicions – you're a detective, after all. But I think you realise now you can trust me.'

I drag myself out of the pull of her ambience and climb to my feet, stretched joints cracking like automatic rifle fire. 'Lady, I don't have to trust nobody.'

'Except, Mister Rainbow, I strongly suspect that in my case you already do.'

We're moving in tight formation along the boulevard – Roarer, Monica and me – and our way takes us past familiar territory. The crime scene's been cleaned up, all ready for the next one. The coppers have gone – taking their blue-and-white tape and trestle horses with them – and the blood's been mopped up so nice that an innocent bystander might imagine it never existed. The window of the dry cleaner's has already been replaced on the insurance.

There's no one outside Monica's apartment block, but I didn't expect there to be, the wheelchair ramp's still *in situ* and the security grille's still in place. The little green buttons that give the residents the opportunity to attract or repel boarders are still all present and correct, and yet . . .

I shrug off the and-yets. Ours not to reason why, ours but to see the case to its conclusion.

We get ourselves to Lulu's.

Tattooists are the Leonardo da Vincis of the 21st century, creating works of art in impossible-to-get-at places. There are plenty up the Cross, but Lulu was the pin man I was after. Yet again, I'm too late.

Some jokers warrant a place in the *Horrible's Cark it, Park it and Mark it* department, the section up the back near the comics they call the *Obituaries*. But not Lulu. He was lowlife and the *Horrible* doesn't recognise lowlife; it's too busy with more serious issues like the Recipe of the Week, celebrity divorce settlements and what socialite's on drugs. Accordingly, for the finer details on the passing of the tattooist, I've got to rely on Aunt Rube.

'He was fed a shiv.'

'His head wasn't blown off?' That's the M.O. I was looking for.

'Use your brain, Rainbow, if you still possess one after that dame's been at it. If you're looking for a similar modus operandi to the one used on Tommy Tycho, you're forgetting that Annabel Franklin was dispatched in much the same way that Lulu was.'

There's a crackle over the wire, but we're both using dead-men's terror-phones, so the dialogue's as safe as such things can be – until the time when it's not.

'The perp was looking for a death, not trying to create a pattern. He didn't blow anyone's head off on the boat, did he? We're not looking at the means now, we're looking at the end.'

I see what she's saying. 'When did Lulu cop it?'

'All I know is it was after closing time.'

So the ink slinger's was shut when it happened, just like it is now. But that's no guarantee nobody's home. While Roarer and Monica keep their eye on the locale, I consider the façade. The cops have come and gone. There's a piece of tape on the door, a ladies' hairdresser specialising in Brazilians on one side, and a strip joint on the other. Photographs depicting the late Master's work litter the window – flying horses leap over beautiful corpses, wreaths of elaborate floral arrangements decorate the corpses of dogs, and there are the usual dragons, skulls, guns, knives, scimitars and Memories of Mother.

I hammer on the door. No answer. I kick at the door. Still no answer.

The hatchway gives to a bit of encouragement from the shoulder and I make my way in, closely followed by Monica, Roarer and the alarm system, gat at the ever-ready.

You seen one tattoo parlour, you seen them all. Pretty pictures line the walls and more pretty pictures grace the books on the window seat, the ones with black covers on them. I flip through the tomes looking for a clue, but all I find is more memories of mothers when I'd like to forget my own, plus dragons and snakes and wild animals, and more dames – all in more or less the state they were born in, only older. There's a clinical air about the place. The lingering pork belly burning smell reminds me how portraits make their way onto people's skin, while the faint sweet-and-sour stench of blood, and the police artist's outline on the floor, reminds me why we're here in the first place.

The police artist was no Leonardo, but the drawing he's done is enough to tell me the corpse still possessed a head when it got that way. Like Rube said, it wasn't a modus operandi the killer was after, just another death.

At the back of the studio I find a nice big chrome machine with a needle hanging off it, followed by a sink, a couch – and the inevitable door to the little dark room out the back.

The room's got a lavatory in it.

It also contains a kid.

The lavatory doesn't tell me a thing.

Neither does the kid.

I recognise him by the pink-and-white tracksuit and the tatts, together with the marks on his skinny white arms, the skinny joker I first met in the vicinity of the corpse in the gutter, and after that in the eating house with the tablecloths just up the road. The drug-addled number who thought I could get him methamphetamines just on the strength of the way I dress. The kid that let himself into this joint when he heard of his master's death, only to shoot up afterwards on whatever he could find, plus uncut grief.

'Who's this joker when he's at home?'

I remove the tourniquet and the needle. He doesn't wake. 'I'd say he's already at home.'

Monica slaps the kid's face and his pinpoint eyes flicker.

I shove her aside and lean over him. 'Where did your boyfriend Lulu keep his books?'

They all keep records. No one thinks they do, everyone imagines it's all nice and anonymous, that when they get *I LOVE JOE* inscribed on their fanny no one will ever know. Except, of course, for Joe – plus all the boyfriends and girlfriends that come after. But the tattoo merchants have got to be ready for the health people when they pay a visit. There's also the Goods and Services Tax, along with every other mercenary in this town that wants a piece of the action.

'What books?' He's got his weight on one needle-tracked paw and he's rubbing his slapped cheek with the other, pretending all the while he's as silly as he looks – at the same time as he's imagining I'm going to fall for it.

'Your boyfriend's book, stupid. The records. The book with all the names in it, including the chart of your own pilgrim's progress.'

The kid looks like he's set on remaining intransigent. But that's before Roarer taps him with his crutch. He cringes, and says exactly what you'd imagine he'd say, which is, 'Don't hit me!' His squinty eyes clear as he recognises me. 'Hey, it's you! Look, man, I'll tell you what you want to know if you'll give me some – I don't care what, just give me anything!'

'I'll give you something all right if you don't tell me what I want to know.' I haul back the footwear. 'Where's the book?'

At first I think he's shaking his wasted head but then I realise he's pointing it and that's when I shelve the gat and rip up the square of blue-and-white lino he's shaking his head at and haul up the floorboard that's under it. Eventually I find it, an exercise book not unlike Imogene's, except that, unlike my daughter's, this one contains a lot of names, dates and illustrations. I leaf through until I find what I'm after, the reason Lulu was exxed before he told anyone what he knew.

Only whoever exxed Lulu overlooked one important fact. And that is that dead men do tell tales. It's just a matter of finding the book they tell them in.

Chapter 36
HERE COMES A CHOPPER . . .

The tattooist's phone's still functioning, which is more than the tattooist is.

'It's No-Name here.' Rube knows who it is and I got no time for the niceties. 'I need a check done – description and form of one Percy James Gardener-with-an-e.'

Nothing fazes Rube. 'By the sound of things you need the information yesterday.'

'Make it the day before.'

When I hang up, I check out my companions. Roarer's nervous and Monica's even more beautiful than when I last looked – the paint shop bloke would probably describe her cheek colour as *Dawn Gloss* – but the pallor on the junkie's face has turned to junket, so I call in the mercenaries.

'St Vincent's casualty? I got you a client. Details as follow: junkie; male of the species; age sixteen or so, going on a hundred; currently hugging the floorboards in Lulu's Pin Parlour.' I give the address. 'Temperature 39, sweating like an oil pump, and inflamed trackline advises serious infection. Prognosis: If you can't do the ambulance in five, make it a hearse.'

'Your name, sir?'

They always want your name. They reckon it's for the records. Tell that to the snoops.

'Look, pal, having a name won't keep this kid alive, while shutting up and getting on with the job just might.'

We're out in the nice, clean ambience of Bayswater Road – pollution reading in the vicinity of ten out of ten, and that's before you take the air quality into account – and the mean streets are humming with the kind of action that, if this was a compost heap, would turn fresh cabbages into mulch in a microsecond.

'Do you think he did it?' Monica asks me.

I stall for time. 'Do I think who did what?'

'Do you think the person who killed Tycho and Annabel also killed the tattooist?'

We're walking fast, because we got a lot to walk fast for – the ambulance is already screaming around the corner. Tomorrow we got a funeral to attend, and if we hang around breathing this air much longer, that funeral might just turn out to be ours. Apart from which, the tail's swapped the white Impreza with tinted windows for a pale-green Mercedes, also with tinted windows. I know it's him – not because I can see him but because of the way he drives, with oversteer-and-correction to the left like he's holding a gun in the right – and he's lingering on the corner of Victoria and Bent like he's in two minds about continuing the tail – or executing us on the spot and getting it over with.

There's an alley to my right and I head for it. It's the kind of alley that in this part of the world can quickly turn into a dead-end – the kind of dead-end you don't come out of except in a body bag, the sort of place they flog filched flat-screen televisions, hot DVDs, and purloined grave-digging equipment – and the pale-green Merc is coming our way like the driver's suddenly not in two minds any longer.

I barrel Roarer and Monica into a fast food franchise just as machine-gun Charlie lets loose with a fusillade.

The blatts are right – there's too much violence in the Cross and the sooner they do something about it the better. Meanwhile innocent bystanders like us just have to do the best we can under the circumstances.

'Do you want fries with that?'

Another volley rat-tats into the window as Monica cranes for a geek at the perpetrator.

'Those dark windows – I can't see anything!'

'You're not supposed to. Get down!'

I cram Monica under a table and work my way out of the shattered doorway just as the Mercedes swings into another laneway. I jam on the hat, haul out the gat, and chuck the hoofs into overdrive. I head off after the Mercedes – past the shoeshine parlour and the real estate con merchant's and yet another strip joint – until I find myself deep in the shadows of Temporary Lane, where I come across the Mercedes in a too-close-encounter with a joker collecting garbage.

'Idiot!'

I can't see the shooter but I see the results. It's Greta Garbo's famous last words as the gunman unloads him into the great rubbish tip in the sky.

After that, the shooter makes himself even scarcer than he was before.

The good thing about tin cans is that not even madmen are going to steal them. The bad thing is that they do five miles per honorarium – which is *why* madmen don't steal them – and that's what we're doing as we head along South Dowling towards the autobahn.

Dead-man's mobile *número dix* does a ring-a-ling.

'I got the information you requested.' Rube's voice is calm. 'The name belongs to a joker they call the Backpacker, a man with a scar on his face resulting from a duel over an unpaid debt. Backpacker's never done time. Repeat, *never done time.* So there's nothing on him locally, nothing with Interpol, nothing anywhere. Apart from any tattoo he might now possess – he's clean. Last seen gunning for our mutual friend over a woman. Physical as follows.'

For *our mutual friend* read Tommy Tycho, and the more Rube talks the more I know I'm in possession of enough facts to bust this case wide open.

'I got one last chore for you,' I say.

The connection crackles. 'Shoot.'

So I shoot and what I shoot is a request to send out invitations to a funeral.

'Deal me date, place and time of funeral – plus the name of the corpse. In code, of course.'

I tell her what she wants to know and after I shelve the communicator I throw a shooftee in the rear-vision and what I see is pretty much what I expect to see, and that is the poky nose of what I know is yet another stolen vehicle – this time a black BMW – going nice and slow like it's a family and the family dog, looking forward to a nice Sunday picnic on a weekday. Except I can't see either the family or the dog. Because, one, they don't exist but also because, two, the windows are painted – in a shade that the paint dudes would probably call *Cutout Delight*.

'Scar on face,' Rube advised me, 'physical as follows . . .'

There's a kids' show on the Tonka's wireless and it's playing one of those all time favourites:

'Oranges and lemons, say the bells of St Clements.
'When will you pay me? say the bells of Old Bailey.
'When I grow rich, say the bells of Shoreditch.
'Here comes a candle to light you to bed,
'And here comes a chopper . . .'

Chapter 37
... TO CHOP OFF YOUR HEAD

It's tomorrow.

I've spent a bad night going over the scenario, and I'm still going over the scenario as we head for the hills.

Orange, the Widow told me – she was going to paint the joint orange.

Monica senses my urgency. 'Can't this thing go any faster?'

I shrug the shoulders that are supporting the Heckler. 'If this thing went any faster, I'd join Roarer in believing in miracles. Slugs can't fly.'

'If they come out of the business end of an equaliser, they can.'

Why does this dame continue to surprise me? Aunt Rube would have the answer to that. *Because you're in love,* she'd say. *And it's a well-known fact, little recorded, that when jokers are in love, they don't see with the eyes of ordinary men, but with eyes that have a large part of a mortuary in them.*

I glance in the rear-vision. Monica's in it. So is our follower's latest conveyance, a black Beamer.

'Where did you learn to talk like that?'

'From my dad, for a start.'

'And for a finish?'

'I've been spending more time with you than could possibly be healthy for a growing girl.'

It's two-fifty-five in the post-meridian. Happy Hour's slated for three. We can hear them doing the warm-up as we approach.

The Widow showed me the menu, which is how I know they picked Brahms' *Voluntary and Fugue*, to be followed by *Nearer My God To Thee*, and after that *Just a Closer Walk with Whosit*, *The Holy Thingummy*, *A Walk in the Park with the Old Boy*, the *Ave* – always the *Ave* – plus *How Great* et cetera, with a grand finale of *Give Me That Old Time Religion*. Toe-tapping favourites that are always going to knock ditties like *Oranges and Lemons* into a gum tree.

When Rube sent out the invites, everyone would have come running. The car park's standing-room only – with black duco in the ascendant – as Roarer eases the Tonka up towards the church on the hill, with the BMW following. Because there's no room at the inn, I get Roarer to poke the 121 around the corner of the prayer house next to the Caddie, and when Roarer decants himself he's in a mood to stay with the wheels. Me and the dame make our way towards the church, leaving Roarer beside the Caddie like a lovestruck Romeo.

The corpse gate – also known as a lych gate – is a bunch of stone and lattice and fairy weed perched a couple of body lengths from the western entry to the praying house. It's the place where they park the coffin until the mourners are ready to take receipt of it, a place of repose. But I got no time for repose.

I swing round to Roarer. 'You coming?'

'I'll join youse in a tick.'

That leaves just me and Monica – plus whoever's going to follow us out of the Beamer. I check the gat's in place and start in on the approach.

It's a nice church if you happen to like churches – a lot of expensive windows and baa-relief over a foe-gothic doorway saying: *GIVE YOUR ALL TO GOD AND YOU'LL BE RICHLY REWARDED.*

I pretend to retie the whitesides while I check out the interior. In the smoky light, made that way by all the *fenêtres*, a black-garbed congregation is peering up at a bunch of organ tubes staring right back at them – unseen eyes behind dark slits, an elongated army of Ned Kellys. The piano player's knocking out the voluntary and fugue but I'm not hearing church music – only the echoes of the song I heard on the Tonka's wireless, and its ramifications.

Oranges and . . .

Hamstring Harry's got pole position on account of the leg, and strung out beside him in no particular order are the distinctive forms of Howard 'Fast One' Hardie, the starting price bookie; king of the smoky poker parlour, Quick Draw Pete Davelo; Jackie the Pimp; Moses Johnstone, the slow drugs maestro; usurer Jock McAddock; plus a bunch of hairstyles lined up in the back pew generally belonging to the two-wheeler set – cats' tails, possums' tails, beavers and plaits . . .

Don't ask me why, but I've a funny feeling as me and Monica get ourselves along an aisle that's crowded on both sides by the assembled thuggery, while the organ pumper belts out *Nearer My God To Thee* – any closer and we'd all be humping tombstones.

They're the names on the list – names I gave Rube plus the ones I checked out personal and then some – all names that possessed larger-than-death-sized motives for exxing Lover Boy.

We come to bury Tycho, not to praise him.

Fixer Murdoch. Flame-haired Annie 'Six-Gun' Tenschyle – pronounced Tan-schoolie, if you know what's good for you. Sensitive Sam, the homicidal maniac. Pete Scissorhands.

All persons that Tommy Tycho at some point in his non-illustrious career crossed, in a way that most people only manage once.

Genuflecting Jennie, Stan the Man, Hieroglyphics Bosch the forger, Hitman Harry 'The Hedgerow' Harvey, a bunch of killers known as The Goon Show, Lightfingers Whitman, a lug that's got a reputation for turning people into stone, the Concrete-Mixer, Prostitute Pete . . .

All persons that for one reason or another wanted to see the arse end of Tommy Tycho.

The light softens the scene like a halo as me and Monica make our way to the altar in the embrace of music that's as soft as the fudge my grandmother used to make, and about as good for anyone's health. The organ grinder might be playing *Hymn to a Massacre*. You can touch the glory, see the heavenly light, hear the celestial music, *taste* the incense. But the smell of the hate that permeates the place trumps all.

Chapter 38
THE UNLOVED ONE

The hate's as tangible as the sandstone steps under the gothic archway, dark as the rafters looming overhead, hard as a bullet, and deep as the grave beneath the tombstone awaiting the contents of the hearse. Which right this moment is pulling up outside. And all heads jerk around at the sound of it. The Dentist. Karrybag. Pig. And in the far corner of the front pew, her face in shadow, someone I'd prefer never to see again this side of Hell – Pandora.

It's more like Dante's central circle of the nether-life than a church, more a collection of the archangel Azrael's followers than a congregation, Fate instead of a funeral. All covered in ethereal light, the kind of colour that generally accompanies an inferno.

The preacher appears out of the door to the chancel. He's exchanged his gravedigger's gear for his preacher's canonicals and his arms are raised like bats' wings. Me and Monica sidle in beside the Widow, turning just in time to see four black-clad goons under the pointy doorway, a coffin teetering on their over-developed *trapezia* as the organ grinder swings into the strains of *The Death March*.

Even through the rosewood lid I can smell it, the pong of the decomposing body that's been parked too long in the kitchen at the Widow's joint, a stench that no one in their right mind would voluntarily suspirate. Except that very few here gathered could be described as being in their right mind.

All eyes are fixed on the coffin and all minds are on the dead man inside it – the corpse of the bastard that took their women, dobbed them into the fuzz, and nicked their ill-gotten gains from under their schnozzes. And never got done for any of it. Who while so doing managed to slip through the interstices of the law, and who right now looks like he's in process of escaping his victims' individual and collective fury forever.

As the rosewood coffin with brass trimmings reaches the halfway mark – little more than an eight-legged silhouette, a giant spider – a figure appears in the doorway behind it, wreathed in black. It's poised like it's on a fleeting visit, like it's only come to see the body into the grave before departing – an anonymous figure: black cloak reaching from the top of its head right down to the church step, hands hidden within loose sleeves, and something, by my reckoning, concealed in the folds of the cloak. It's like an avenging angel, but it's also like it's not here – on account of no one, with the exception of me, is paying it any attention.

Instead, all eyes are on the coffin, borne aloft by the corpse-carriers. Who carefully lower the box onto the plinth in front of the preacher. Before turning to face the figure in the doorway and the congregation.

The main man raises his arms. 'Praise be to all of us gathered here together.'

'Amen!'

'Lest our light be dimmed before our time, let us each and every one of us be prepared to be taken at any moment.'

'Amen!'

'Light of light, heart of hearts, soul of souls.'

'Amen, amen, amen!'

The preacher's eyes linger on the gathering. 'Welcome.' His face is full of benevolence. 'Before burial, a short commercial break.' He smiles. 'I just want to say that the Hillbilly Church is a fine new establishment and in it we worship God Almighty in a fine new way. No matter what your sins, the Hillbilly Church is the way to salvation. Even after you die, under the auspices of the Hillbilly Church, you can expect to go on living. All it takes is a little bit of giving.'

But a certain impatience accompanies his words.

'Get on with it, mate, we're here to see the bastard buried!'

'Very well. But first, is there anyone here present who would like to say a eulogy?'

At this point the figure at the back of the church, poised for flight, unaccountably hesitates.

Pig then clambers to his trotters and turns in the confines of his pew hole to eyeball his brothers. 'Yeah, I would.' It isn't in the script, but that doesn't stop it happening. 'This bastard dudded me good, the way he dudded everyone else here.' He's forgotten his expensive education and instead is saying what he thinks. It doesn't make what he says any prettier. 'He robbed me of money but worst of all he stole my self-respect. I hated the bastard then, and I hate him now. I don't get many happy days in my life, but this is one of them.'

He resumes his seat and after that it's the Dentist's turn, then Karrybag's. But it's when it's Psycho Harrigan's turn – Psycho Harrigan with the scar on his schnozz that Tycho brought about, courtesy of a whip – that the script takes a turn for the worse. Unlike the rest, Psycho's thinking outside the box.

'How do we know there's even a body in there?' he says. The seed's been planted and there's a general murmur of assent. 'All right, let's say there *is* a body. Anyone got a bit of paper that says it's Tycho's?'

There's action in the doorway, but there's more action beside me. The Widow's got to her feet and is about-facing the doubters. Tough little nut, this Widow. Silence falls over the congregation.

'For those that aren't aware of the fact, I'm the Widow Tycho.' She's no longer the person that gave up her place at the butcher's. 'If anyone knows my husband, it's me. Haven't I been his loving spouse since I was a girl? Haven't I lived with his corpse for three days? Didn't I personally see it into the coffin?'

'What about the ID?' someone asks.

The Widow nods her head. 'All right, there aren't any fingerprints to identify him by. But that's only because Tommy never did anything wrong and never did time or was even arrested. Yeah yeah, so there's no head on the body. But there's still the tattoo that says people like to be deceived and that Tommy's deceived them.' She glares around. 'It's got to be him. Who else could it be?'

It's a big speech, but after that it's my turn. I don't like public speaking, never have. I'm more a fist-and-gun man than a mouthpiece. But sometimes you got to do it, and this is one of those times. So I climb to my feet and face the music. The organ grinder stops as I turn. I'm still facing the music. Most of the jokers know me and most of the jokers that know me don't like me, because I'm on the other side of the ledger from the column most of them occupy. But I got their attention. The only movement comes from the doorway as the cloaked figure makes what appear to be minor adjustments to its cloak. But that's before there's another movement beside the figure. I ignore it.

'I realise that,' I begin, 'to all present, time is a precious commodity. Life might not be, but time is.' I send the peepers on a tour of the pews. 'But there's someone not present.'

'Yeah, Tycho.'

The observation raises a laugh, but I'm not interested in laughs. I haul out the book. 'This is the records from Lulu's Pin Parlour. You all knew Lulu.' I open the book. It's a nice exercise book in the old style with a green cover, the sort that's got a little white patch on the front to put your name and address in. The space is blank but the pages aren't. I got one eye on the book and the other on the doorway.

'I draw your attention to the following entry.' If anyone knows what's coming they don't show it. 'The entry concerns someone known to most of you by the moniker Percy James Gardener.' I keep my voice casual. 'Some of you knew him as the

194

Backpacker, a small-time gambler that was part-time innocent backpacker, but like most of you here present was actually a full-time rogue.'

I got their attention. The doorway hasn't.

'All his life, just like Tycho, Gardener managed to evade the law. He existed on the edge of crime, but that didn't mean he was apart from it. Recently, just like the rest of you, he was gunning for Tycho. But can anyone see him here?' There's a general shaking of heads. 'That's because two things happened to prevent him. One, Tycho crossed one person too many, and so for the first time in Tycho's life, Sydney got too hot for him. And, two, Gardener crossed Tycho.'

'So what happened?' someone yells.

I let them have it between the eyes. *No one killed Tycho.* Instead, Tycho killed Gardener. After warning his girlfriend he was in danger, he drugged Gardener and took him to Lulu's, where he got the pin man to write an inscription on the Backpacker's neck.

'After that, with the help of a random space cadet, he took Gardener down the road and blew his head off. No head and no recorded prints meant there was means of identification. Apart from the tattoo, which of course told everyone who wanted to know that the body belonged to Tycho.'

It takes a while for it all to sink in but when it does it leads to the inevitable question.

'So who's in the coffin?'

I let them work it out for themselves.

'It's gotta be Gardener!'

That leaves something else to work out.

'SO WHERE'S TYCHO?'

I don't nod towards the back of the praying house because if I nod towards the back, the figure in black with Roarer riding shotgun – and thereby stopping it either drawing its gun or escaping – is going to die of more bullets than anyone has ever died of before. I nod to Roarer to get Tycho the hell out of there. But I'm mistaken regarding two important factors.

One: I've overestimated Roarer's brainpower.

And two: I've underestimated the power of hate.

These insane bastards are here to witness the funeral of Tommy Tycho and no one – repeat, no one – is going to deprive them of it.

'That's the bastard up the back!'

Chapter 39
DEATH OF A LADIES' MAN

I don't know what I thought was going to happen on this nice winter's day in this nicest of all praying establishments. But it turns out everyone in the congregation is packing a shooter, and suddenly they're waving them around. There's Benellis and Berettas and Frommers and Rugers and Heckler & Kochs, even the odd Hotchkiss – commonly known as *The Hotchkiss of death*. The air that's tinted courtesy of the church windows becomes as full of lead as a hole in the ground belonging to Mount Isa Mines or BHP Billiton. It gives a whole new meaning to the word *leadlight*.

Tommy Tycho thought he was safe. He's been following us – even taking the odd potshot, as well as threatening the lives of everyone on the *Wooden No* – because he was determined to see his last con out to the end. He wanted to attend his own funeral. His wish is in process of being granted.

Roarer's made himself scarce, while the preacher's yelling and the Widow's trying to push past Monica only she can't because Monica's got hold of her by her arm. Monica's not about to let go in a hurry, even as the pointy-topped gothic windows come down around our lugs and the figure in the doorway – Mediflex-gloved hands clutching its elephant gun – jerks about like a man possessed.

Only he's not a man possessed, he's just Tommy Tycho, who's miraculously come to life again, and I'm certain of that fact because – when his arms come up and the cloak of anonymity finally falls away forever – I can see the ring-a-ring-a-rosy conformation of the infamous tattoo around his neck. The tattoo that says everyone in the joint except Tycho is an idiot. But that's not what the new script says. Because when Tycho's reborn it's only for the briefest of seconds. And after those briefest of seconds he's nothing more than a lifeless body clutching a gun under the caption above the doorway that says GIVE YOUR ALL TO GOD AND YOU'LL BE RICHLY REWARDED – why does it look like *retarded* – his body, his hopes and the new head he's grown full of sweetmeats.

I turn away and gesture to the organ grinder. He nods back at me and begins hammering out the next item on the menu– *Just a Closer Walk With Thee*. Roarer meanwhile has appeared in the doorway again, and is busy slamming a couple of slugs out of his crutch rifle into the chandelier to get everyone's attention.

In the relative silence, I take up the refrain. 'Jesus grant it is my plee-ee-ea.'

Voice played a big part in Aunt Rube's curriculum – how to use it, how to throw it, how to play it – and it's like the congregation suddenly remembers where they are, as a couple of willing and ready volunteers drag the newly-minted corpse of Tommy Tycho up the aisle, past the wreckage of the light attachment and the crunching remnants of the windows, and dump it on the already-occupied coffin. The gats find their way back into their respective hidey-holes and the hymn books come out as the piano player leads the way into the chorus, and one by one the voices of the celebrants climb into the music alongside.

Surreal? You bet, but that's Sydney town for you. Everyone seems happy, or as happy as they'll ever be, and they're settling into the singing real nice, and to settle them still further, I give them *Ave Maria* in the original Latin, the way it should be sung:

Ave Maria, gratia plena/ Dominus tecum/ Benedicta Tu in mulieribus/ Et benedictus fructus ventris.

It shuts them up for a while, and after I reckon it's safe, with the clergyman shivering like he's in a paroxysm of disbelief, and the pianist still hammering away and the little Ned Kelly masks in the organ pipes giving with the chords like they're loving every minute of it, the congregation raises its collective voice to heaven, and segue into everyone's all-time favourite, taking the organist along for the ride:

'Lord my God, when I in awesome wonder . . .'

I give Roarer the nod and he underarms the crutch that doubles as a gat and hops up the aisle. While the congregation is otherwise employed, we escort the Widow to the door to the chancel. The congregation's too involved with the hymn singing to notice.

'I see the stars,

'I hear the rolling thunder

'Thy power throughout the universe displayed . . .'

The criminal element of Sydney is right in the swing of it now. They're back in their miserable childhoods peering into some dim-lit crevice of their souls, while I'm still giving with the big brassies as I head out after the others.

'Then sings my soul, my Saviour God to Thee
'How great Thou art, How great Thou art . . .'
I don't wait to see what happens after that. Wait to see what happens after that and I've got to face more music than I care to face right now, namely a bunch of heavily-armed hoods that might suddenly remember they don't like me all that much, not to mention the avenger in black at the far end of the front row, who of all those assembled would have little or no interest in Tommy Tycho – only in me, and the possibility of making a trifecta of the occasion: Pandora.

Roarer's already in the vestry while Monica follows with the Widow. I bring up the rear as we head for the interstice between a kirk and a hard place, the church and the McMansion, the place where the Caddie's ready for the getaway.

'She got enough gas in her?'

Roarer's waving a length of garden hose and nodding towards the car park as he climbs in behind the wheel. 'Those babies won't be going anywhere in a hurry, but we will.'

'What about you, Roarer?' I glance back at the church. 'You reckon you're going to make it to heaven after this little lot?'

'After what little lot?'

'Oh, you know, being ultimately responsible for the death of Tommy Tycho – I mean if you hadn't been there he could have escaped – plus sacrilege, blasphemy, impiety, profanity, desecration and probably simony, not to mention robbing the church of a car.'

Roarer shrugs. 'I reckon I've given the church more than it ever gave me. Apart from which, all those potential sign ups has got to put me back in the black.'

Roarer's maths produces a silence that's broken only by the flap of the wings of God's starlings and the buzz of God's bees. Add to that the syncopated bellow of a bunch of crooks busy demanding the return of that old-time religion while the bullet-spattered corpse of Tommy Tycho – the man that was already dead but has just died some more – lies atop the coffin of his victim.

I always find something moving about a second passing.

At last the Caddie takes off past the tombstones and all the de-gassed getaway cars – including the stolen Beamer. We say goodbye to the nice little church with its windows all shot up – plus the roar of Sydney's crème de la crime yelling *Gimme That Old-time Religion* like it's some kind of a stick-up. But I'd prefer that we moved just that little bit faster, just to make sure we get out of here in a different manner to the one Tycho did.

'Step on it!' I tell Roarer.

We're not in the Tonka car, so he steps on it.

Chapter 40
NEVER TRUST A DAME

Me and Monica are in the speakeasy and we got the *Daily Terrorgraph* spread out between us. Monica's perched on the other side of the tableau and she's still got blue eyes and she's also still more beautiful than she's got any right to be.

'So how did you know?' she asks me.

I shrug. It settles the gat. 'I first got suspicious when I was handed that list of suspects – free, gratis and for nothing.'

'Suspicious of what?'

'Of lists in general, and of the death of Tommy Tycho in particular.'

'Why?'

'I knew Tycho.'

'And after that?'

I put on my Jimmy Cagney look, the one where he grapefruits the dame. Only I haven't got a grapefruit, so all I'm left with is the look. 'Listen, I'm the one asking the questions. And my first question is: who are you? And don't tell me you're the daughter of a war veteran in the habit of smuggling military-issue weapons out of Afghanistan, because even the Australian army doesn't arm people with anachronistic bangers made in Turkey all of sixty years ago.' I hunch the shoulders. 'So how did you really come by the gat?'

It's Monica's turn to shrug. 'The way anyone gets anything these days – at a price and on the black market. It saves a lot of paperwork, and you don't have to pay the Goods and Services Tax.'

That answers some of the question. I ask the rest of it. 'Having figured the gun, I also figured there wasn't a war hero father who also happened to be – so help me – a cross-dressing, depressive transsexual. So I return to my original question: who are you, how come the apartment – and what's with the wheelchair I donated to the cabbie?'

When Rube checked who owned Monica's apartment, she came up with a lot of mumbo jumbo about holding companies and straw men and third parties and John Does – and nothing at all about who actually held the title to it.

She sighs. 'The apartment – like most things in this town – belongs to an insurance company, and so do I. Insurance companies are like banks – they own property the way people like you and I own debts. The apartment belonged to a workers' compensation fraudster and the wheelchair was part of the fraud. The fraudster got a jail term while the company got the apartment, and contents.'

'Plus you?'

'Yeah, you might say they got me, too. Like you, Mister Rainbow, I started out as a private investigator. Except that somewhere along the line I sold out. I now investigate insurance fraud.' She plays with her whisky sour. 'It's big business, insurance fraud. Again just like the banks, my company avoids unnecessary payouts. They've been onto the Tychopouloses ever since a new salesman inadvertently gave them a cheap rate on Tommy – remember, he was relatively young and he was also clean – with the wife as sole beneficiary. We knew they were up to something, only we didn't know what. So the company set me up in the apartment they'd come in possession of, situated just above that of Tycho's girlfriend.'

Annabel Franklin. The dame I owed a debt to. Who called me in on the strength of my calling card thinking I could help, after her lover said someone was out to kill him. Information that Annabel was supposed to take to the police but came to me with instead.

'But then three things happened. One: someone got killed. Two: Annabel was murdered. And three: you turn up on my doorstep like an avenging angel.' She tries a smile. It comes out a grimace. 'Requiring me to keep a close eye on you, because you were going to do my dirty work for me – exposing the Tycho scam at the same time as you were looking for Annabel's killer.' She reaches across the table and her hand lights on mine like a death wish. 'Look, I'm sorry, but it's my job.'

I shift the fist and the wish list falls on the tableau.

'So you're a P.I. that found the easy way out, making sure the little man goes on losing while the big boys keep rolling in clover. And meanwhile you been in the game so long you carry your own insurance – in the form of Naloxone and Flumazenil, plus any other accessories that might save you from the depredations of strangers.'

The nickelodeon's on playback and the tune it's playing is *Wooden Heart*. Elvis is busy telling the world to treat him nice, treat him good, treat him like it really should, while Monica Best looks at me with what a casual bystander might take to be sadness. The beautiful peepers are still blue, but now there's an emptiness in them, like a cloud's just covered the sun and a cold winter's day just got that much colder.

'But, please,' she says eventually, 'tell me how *you* knew.'

'Knew what?'

She waves a beautiful hand at the story in the *Terror* that's telling anyone who cares that the cops have cracked the mystery of who killed Tommy Tycho, that it's out of the *Cold Case* basket and into the one marked *Too Easy*. The rag also reports that there was a funeral, and that a number of colourful Sydney identities were present, and that it was a moving occasion – moving, that is, in that Loverboy Tycho was finally moved to his final resting place.

She takes a deep breath. 'How you knew that the corpse in the kitchen wasn't Tycho's. How you knew . . .' She fidgets. 'I'm sorry but I need this information in order to make out a report for my employers.'

I've got nothing to gain by withholding, only more sadness than the sadness I already got. 'Everyone was keen for that corpse to belong to Tommy Tycho – so keen they conveniently ignored facts that were staring them in the face. And the facts staring them in the face were that the tattoo was the sole identifier. There was no head and no one had ever taken Tycho's dabs, leaving nothing but the tattoo. A tag around the neck of a goose saying it's a duck don't make it a duck.'

Chapter 41
ORANGES AND LEMONS

'Tycho was a worm and a dobber,' I continue, 'a sneak and a creep, a phantom in a world of ghosts. He was quicker on his tootsies than Cassius Clay and never got caught for so much as non-payment of fare on the 339 to Clovelly.'

'So when did you realise he wasn't the corpse?' Monica asks.

'I just happen to know Latin. And when I looked at the neck at the Widow's I knew the inscription didn't conform to the original. It was meant to read: *Populus vult decipi decipiatur* – "The people wish to be deceived, so deceive them". A neat little quote for someone that spent the whole of his life on the con.' I shrug. 'But the last word on the neck of the corpse in the kitchen wasn't *decipiatur* but *decapitare* – no longer "so let them" but "let's do a beheading". Someone had altered the lyrics. The ink slinger wouldn't have known Latin from lantana, which meant the person who did the switch *must* have been Tycho. Tattoos aren't like Words for Windows, where you hit *Delete* and everything trundles off to *Recycle.* If you want to alter a tattoo, you got to find yourself a new canvas. Which meant the new words had to have been on somebody else's cutaneous tissue. It turned out to be Tycho's last joke.'

She nods. It's the sort of nod that et cetera and et cetera.

'You gave me a clue when you said no one buzzed in order to gain entry to Annabel's apartment. A lover's always got the key to the apartment of his *inamorata*. After Tycho killed Annabel, he just had time before I rocked up to type into her computer a list of persons that hated him enough to kill him, a nice little bunch of red herrings designed to send the cops on a wild-goose chase, if they were in the business of chasing. All I needed to do after that was identify the corpse. When Tycho realised that, he did away with the tattooist. When Lulu copped it, I knew why. And after the junkie – the kid who helped Tycho set up the rube for the shooting – pointed me to the book, I knew who belonged to the new canvas. For Tycho, the beauty about Gardener was that – like Tycho himself – he had no form. Like Tycho, there were no records to link his dabs to. Knowing the cops would run dead on the case, all Tycho had to do was put the identifier around Gardener's neck and ever so carefully blow his head off.'

'You've explained why he killed Gardener and the tattooist, but why Annabel? Annabel did nothing wrong apart from coming to you. And that's not enough to kill anyone for.'

'Think about it. There was a deal between a man afraid for his life, and his wronged wife. For once, this wronged wife had the upper hand. Sure she was getting a cut of the insurance but she wanted more: she wanted the girlfriend dead.'

Monica frowns. It's a beautiful frown. 'You said there was a final clue.'

This is the bit I like, the bit that puts the final coat of gloss on the case. 'There's no paint colour that goes by the name *orange*.'

'Meaning?'

'At the Merry Widow's I came across a piece of paper with a lot of crossing-out on it and right down the bottom the word *orange*. When I asked the Widow what it meant, she fed me some story about the joint needing painting.' I shrug. 'Two problems with that. One, if you're trying to flog real estate in this town, you don't paint it orange. And two, no such hue exists in any paint company's repertoire. So the Widow's not-so-white lie tied her into the jig. And the rest, as they say, is history.'

Monica looks up from her note taking. 'So what – in context – did the word *orange* mean?'

I kick the record player and the xylophone switches to something with *heartbreak* in it. 'To qualify for a payout from your insurance company, the Tychos had to "prove" the corpse was Tommy's. The fingerprints didn't matter because neither Tommy nor Gardener possessed any – at least not as far as anyone was concerned. The big identifier, therefore, was the tattoo around his neck, and the major counter identifier was the head. That meant Tycho had to blow off the head – while at the same time leaving the tattoo. Accordingly, they came up with the idea of the elephant gun. After that, all they had to do was experiment with distance – how far the gun had to be in order to take off the head nice and clean, while not affecting the tattoo. Hoping all the while – because it would be that much easier – that Tommy could do it from a distance.

'They experimented with shop dummies, the theft being duly recorded in the newspapers. They tried several paces away, a couple of paces away, and at arm's length – until finally they accepted the inevitable: that Tycho would have to get right up close and personal if he was going to remove the head yet still leave the tattoo in place.'

'And that distance would have been 0-range,' she says.

Monica's voice is soft and sweet but it's her famous last words as far as this defective's concerned. I've paid my debt to Annabel, and I never did have a debt to this dame, unless it's the age-old debt that anyone suffering from blind, abject love owes to the object of his infatuation, after she says the only interest she ever had in you was 'professional'.

Accordingly, I grab my fedora and place it on my head. 'One more question,' I ask. 'Does the Widow get to keep the dough?'

Monica looks up at me and I see that her eyes are no longer beautiful but calculating. 'We'll find some way out of it. We always do.'

With that, I leave the speakeasy, nodding to the kid behind the bar as I enter a world that's got a sky the colour of the dame's eyes when I finally realised she didn't care for me all that much.

Roarer's behind the wheel of the Caddie, all ready to take me to where I should be a lot more than I am. Because I'm not just a private detective, I'm also a dad. And the six- or is it ten-year-old that makes me that way is waiting for me to get on with the long-overdue business of fathering.

Chapter 42
SAVE THE LAST DANCE FOR ME

'One step, two step – higher, higher, that's better – three!' Madame Blavatsky cries. 'Imogene Scutt, concentrate! Pay attention to the music, and what it's *telling* you!'

There aren't too many dance academies left in Sydney. Come to think of it, there's not too much of anything left in Sydney. Not after the wreckers have been at work and all the extortion and rackety by-play that goes by the name of progress has torn down anything that really matters. Not after the great god Dough-Re-Me has nodded from on high and his disciples have put their hands in other people's pockets to pay the dues.

Dance academies are soul and soul has been excised from this burg. All that's left are millions of punters glued to their idiot boxes, ten thousand ant-brown corpses baking on Bondi Beach, a couple of hundred empty minds in parliament house and the hollow uniforms of the fuzz in their ivory tower in College Street pretending to do their dirty work for them.

Correction: there are fragments of soul, the barest silhouette, and it comes courtesy of the likes of Madame Blavatsky. She's striding around the dance floor, her great leotarded form towering over the littlies in ballet pumps – my daughter among them.

'No jewellery, Mary-Jane,' she bellows, 'how many times do I have to tell you? Get rid of those silly dingly-danglies at once, they interfere with your movement!'

The kids struggle to get their leg-warmered legs over the impossibly high barre that runs around the mirrored wall of this great, grey, cavernous room.

'One step, two step, three: that's better!'

Some pirouette – if they're able – their faces set sturdy to the music as the tinkle-tankle of the piano in the corner interprets Tchaikovsky like he's never been interpreted before – sort of ballet in ragtime.

'No, no, no! Stop, stop, stop!'

When I was a kid, Aunt Rube brought me to Madame Blavatsky's to pick up the moves, to learn how to pirouette and come back to earth in a perfect arabesque – in other words how to leap and duck and side dive, the rudiments of the rhythm of movement, especially the *cruciate-ligament pas-de-seul*, the basic step of survival.

'You're moving like a herd of bloody elephants,' Madame Blavatsky says. 'Has anyone here seen an elephant in a tutu?' She allows the titter before cancelling it abruptly with a glance as sharp as a stiletto. 'No? Well, I have.' She waves an arm that's got more grace in it than any prima ballerina in the *Ballet Russe*. 'I've seen it *here*.' She stamps her foot and the earth moves. 'Yes, this is where I've seen it, here and now, as performed by the whole bloody pack of you, in my – *my*, mind you – academy of dance.'

She glares around at the minuscule miscreants. 'And what does it tell me you've learnt? Nothing.

What can you do? Play rugby league football probably, because you certainly can't dance.' She steps back, all two hundred pounds of her light as a feather, and that's when the graceful arm comes out again, first to indicate the piano player, and then to give the Noddy to me.

When you're in Madame Blavatsky's, you do what Madame Blavatsky tells you to do. And right now Madame Blavatsky's telling me to dance – whitesides and all – so, after parking the hat and the gat, that's exactly what I do.

What the kids *should* be seeing is what Madame Blavatsky has just described to them – a bull elephant dancing. But that's not what's before them. As the music of Stravinsky scorches the heights of the ceiling and ricochets off the mirrored wall and echoes through the mean streets outside that right now are turning to blood-dusk, my X-rated musculature responds to the magic of the muse.

There's no bull elephant in the room.

Just Robert Murray Helpmann. Or maybe Rudolf Khametovich Nureyev. The kids sense the wind in the trees, the magic when incredulity flaps its awkward wings and beats a hasty retreat. They see what happens when a miracle occurs and a great lumpy beast of a private detective takes flight in a dusty dance parlour in inner-city Darlinghurst. Finally, they hear the sound when that private detective's bulk lands on the floorboards with the merest whisper of a suspicion, and not even the tiniest mote of dust is disturbed.

The music stops and I bow and return to my place next to Madame Blavatsky.

'*That's* how it's done.' The grand dame glares at her charges yet again. 'That's poetry and that's what I want from you – perfect stanzas, beautiful couplets and the most eloquent of imagery.' She nods in my direction like Eugene Goossens acknowledging the tour-de-force of a principal danseur after a performance worthy of an angel. 'Thank you, Mr Smith, thank you, pianist.' Then she turns back to her downcast flock of fledglings. 'Now, dance, damn you, dance!'

We're making our way back through the mean streets, the kid with stars in her eyes and me with a hole in my cakehole where my back tooth ought to be.

'Wow!' She's still dancing. 'Do you think any of the others have a father like me?'

Her mitt in mine feels like a wasp.

'I doubt it.'

'Do you think they're jealous?'

I shake my head. 'I doubt that, too, sweetheart. In fact, I doubt it a very great deal.'

Because in reality I'm a thug, not the kind of dad who that rolls around on the floor with his daughter and knows what her exam results are and remembers her birthday. What kid in her right mind's going to be jealous of that? But you got to take the rough with the smooth in this world and Immo takes the rough with the rougher and still comes up smiling. I like that in a kid.

Come to think of it, I like that in anyone.

Salina's waiting in the doorway of the dump I bequeathed her after we got ourselves unmarried and I went to live on a boat. The look on her dial-up says it all.

'I suppose I ought to be grateful for small mercies, Rainbow. Specifically, that you brought my little girl home in one piece.' She holds out her arms like she's taking delivery of a decrepit pound puppy. 'Come to me, darling.' The kid comes to her and Salina embraces her, all the while glaring at me like I'm some kind of criminal. 'So what happens now?'

'What always happens, Sal. I dump Imogene with you and then I go back to the boat. After a while, I get a phone call and after that I go out into the big, wide, dangerous world and take yet another tilt at the windmill.'

Sal's not the type to waste valuable time on allusions, literary or otherwise. 'We're still not safe, are we?' The house is behind her but the rest of her life's still in front. 'I mean, all those horrible people you're surrounded with are never going to go away, are they?'

'If you're talking about Tommy Tycho, he's dead and buried. If you're referring to Pandora, it's not you and the kid she's after, it's me. Meanwhile, the rest of the evildoers have more important things on their minds – like prostitution, drugs, extortion and murder.' I check the fedora. There's a bullet hole in the crown I didn't notice before. 'However . . .'

There's always an *however.*

Salina hugs Immo close and kisses the top of

her head. When she looks up her eyes are shining. 'Things aren't going to get any better, are they?'

'Yeah, sure they are, Sal. They'll get a whole lot better – you can rely on it.' I jam the fedora with the hole in it on my skull and turn away, on account of my eyes might have acquired a bit of a gleam in them, too. 'Only you can also rely on the very great probability that first they're going to get a whole lot worse.'

Also in the series

978-1-922057-20-4 (digital)
978-1-922057-45-7 (print)

Winner of silver in the 2012 Independent Publishers Awards.

She's a surgeon, she's beautiful and she desperately wants
Mister Rainbow to shed some light on her husband's past.
But when he does, she wishes he hadn't. Because what Rainbow
discovers is a handless hood – and a whole lot of murders.

Rainbow's a retro private eye who keeps himself to himself.
He lives (illegally) on a boat in Sydney Harbour, has no identity,
and frequents speakeasies. He's also got a nemesis called Pandora …

The Case of the Hood With No Hands, the first novel in the
Mister Rainbow heptalogy, is a modern story with a wink and
a nod to the golden age of pulp fiction. With its memorable
characters, witty dialogue and fast-paced plot, it signals
the arrival of an arresting new Australian talent.

Did you enjoy this book?
Why not tell your followers about it?

www.xoum.com.au